ASGARD'S DRAG

Relinquished

Shrouded

Assigned

Accosted

Destruction

EDITORIAL REVIEW

Thor's Dragon Rider
Book Eight

Accosted

"Fans of fantasy and myth will enjoy this Norse-inspired tale where Thor and his company of friends and dragons attempt to save his half brother from Helheim." Laura K., Proofreader, Red Adept Editing

"In this action-packed installment of the Thor's Dragon Rider series, Thor, along with the Valkyries and their dragons, must stop the Midgard serpent from reaching Asgard and unleashing chaos." Stefanie B., Line Editor, Red Adept Editing

Accosted

Ebook first published in USA in May 2022 by Cosy Burrow Books

Ebook first published in Great Britain in May 2022 by Cosy Burrow Books

www.katrinacopebooks.com

Published by Cosy Burrow Books

ISBN : 978-0-6455102-0-1

❀ Created with Vellum

BLURB

Three deadly children, one mischievous god, and Asgard to save.

The time has come to face Hel. Despite their productive efforts to fill the goddess of Helheim's demands, Kara and her companions have come up short. Still, Odin demands they retrieve Balder at any cost. A peaceful solution is uncovered, if only the quick-to-wrath goddess will accept their offer.

The Midgard serpent is loose on the realms, leaving Thor and the Valkyries unsure where he will turn up next. He leaves destruction in his wake as he searches for Asgard.

On top of dealing with Jormungandr and Hel, Fenrir's tether thins, and the hound is ready to unleash his wrath on Odin. Angering all three siblings at once has been predicted to start Ragnarok.

Chapter One

Murky brown scales ripple under the lake's surface, and black beady eyes rise, stopping just below the water. The Midgard serpent stays protected beneath the waters of Svartalfheim, surveying the dragons flying above. We've followed him through the Yggdrasil, sighting him as he slithered onto the realm. Jormungandr has either taken a wrong turn to Asgard or is up to mischief in the land of the dwarves.

Frosty air pushes against my face, which is speckled with snowdrops. A brilliant blue sky broken by fluffy white clouds reflects off the water. I'm glad it's daytime. When the sun is shining, the dwarves stay secure in their caves. Today, this will protect them not only from the sun, but also from the trouble the serpent will cause. Rumors circulated in Midgard about how the serpent had devoured several villages lining the large lakes and ocean edges.

It takes me a moment to recognize the red darting reflection careening to the left across the water's surface as Tanda. The red dragon's sudden movement catches the attention of Jormungandr, causing him to swivel and follow her progress. The danger to the red dragon and Britta is short-lived when the serpent is distracted by Drogon's brown form as he flies in the opposite direction. The lowness of their flight makes me worried for Britta's and Hildr's safety as they ride their dragon friends. The serpent could project out of the water toward the dragons at any time.

Cloaked in invisibility, Elan hovers not far above the water. Digging my knees into Elan's saddle, I tug at the edges of my dragon-scale cloak. I pull my hood farther over my head to make sure I'm fully covered and also sheathed in invisibility while it protects my numb cheeks from the weather. Despite triple-checking, I still feel exposed, as though those eyes can see me. It makes me twitch on the saddle. Sweat, caused by the tension of the chase coupled with the warmth of the dragon-scale cloak, beads on the back of my neck and trickles down my back under my black leather uniform, stopping just below the coccyx.

Red-faced with anger, Thor stomps along the shoreline framed by tall, snow-capped rocky mountains. Earlier, he was having trouble staying on the saddle when Elan dodged the serpent's attacks. Her sudden jerky movements flung him over her side, leaving him grasping onto her saddle and exposing our position as he fell out of her invisibility. It was already hard enough to keep his bulky form concealed underneath my cloak. Because of this, Elan placed him on the shoreline a little while ago. We didn't want to leave Thor out of the confrontation, but the other dragons opted not to carry him. His heavier form added to the weight of a Valkyrie restricted their reaction time. Lacking the Viking ship, he fumes on the bank, unable to join in the attacks.

A gush of fresh breeze pushes down on me as Naga flits above us with Eir riding on his back. The serpent's eyes follow the slightly smaller dragon's progress. Zildryss peers over Eir's shoulders, eyeing the enormous serpent and licking alternating eyes as he often does when he's pondering something or using his third eye's foresight. Protectively, Elan moves to block the serpent's path to the blue dragon. I admire Elan's heart even though there is no rationality behind her thoughts. Her invisibility isn't going to drag Jormungandr's attention away from Naga and to her. Although, somehow, these beady eyes focus on me again, making me feel as though I must be exposed.

A buildup of ice sticks to the reins, making my palms slip, and I rub it on my leather pants, careful not to let go of the lead in case Elan swerves suddenly. White knuckles poke out from under my sleeve, exposing them. Perhaps the Midgard serpent *can* see me. I yank the end of my sleeve over my fists, feeling the warmth of the cloak gradually trapping around my hands. During our past encounters, I have seen signs of intelligence in the serpent, and Jormungandr has probably recognized the telltale signs that Elan and I are here. My cloak does leave tiny parts of my flesh exposed. Maybe I should find a way to make gloves and a face mask out of dragon scales as well. I'm not sure how well it would work with the hard exterior of the large scales.

I speak to my dragon through our bond. *Elan. Can we please move up higher? Something about the serpent's gaze makes me suspect he can see us. It's making me nervous.*

Elan's body drops and rises a few times in rhythm with her beating wings, and I feel her presence through our bond. *He shouldn't be able to see us. But if it's making you uncomfortable, I'll rise a bit. At least high enough so we can get away in a hurry if he does charge us.*

The few extra feet higher lessens my anxiety and slows my heartbeat to a more manageable level.

Hearing a large thump on the shoreline, I gaze

over to see Thor collecting his hammer from the bank. The redness of his face makes it hard to tell where his hair finishes and his face starts. He still hasn't gotten over his anger from not being with us to fight off Jormungandr. Seeing him stuck on the shoreline makes me wish he had the nifty ship that could fold down into a suitcase. The last time I saw it, Thor had stored it in his carriage. We didn't bring the carriage on this trip, though. We figured traveling without it would be quicker and easier.

When I return my gaze to the water, there is no sign of the serpent. He has descended within the water. More unease rises in my stomach. I wouldn't be surprised if Jormungandr still sees us hovering above, even though we can't see him.

Keeping an eye out for any movement and staying just out of reach, the four large dragons continue to hover higher over the lake's surface where we last spotted the Midgard serpent. Remaining close is the quickest way to attack him. We hope to at least chase him back to Midgard and hinder him from reaching Asgard. Even though Asgard's realm holds few rivers, that wouldn't stop the serpent from traveling there. He can easily cross over land using the few lakes for security and cover, camouflaging him.

Several hundred yards away, a considerable surge

of water explodes from the surface as Jormungandr flicks his tail and swims in the other direction. I'm amazed at the enormousness of the serpent as a few parts of his body become visible through the churned waters of the river on Svartalfheim. He's bigger than many fully grown dragons combined, and doubt rises within me—how could Thor defeat something this big? It's almost like we need help from all of the wasteland dragons to defend us against the serpent. I can't fathom how one god with his hammer and a belt of strength stands a chance.

We follow Jormungandr's progress, trying to determine where he wishes to go, hoping to protect anything the serpent attacks. He continues beneath the water's surface, and my unease intensifies. I sense he's trying to distract us from something important.

With another loud thump, Thor stomps to retrieve his hammer from the shoreline again, his body rigid with annoyance. Elan flies us over to him with a little prompt, turning us visible before landing on the bank.

I smirk, amused by my leader's blotchy red face. "What do you expect this to achieve?"

Thor grumbles, halts his stomping, and thrusts his hands in the air with frustration. "I don't know. I'm hoping the vibration will chase him back to Midgard. There's no use throwing my hammer at him. It could miss and hit one of the dragons. If the vibration doesn't chase him away, then I hope he'll come to the bank and lift his head out of the water so I can attack." He indicates roughly toward the serpent. "He's obviously smart enough to realize this, and it's driving me crazy." Thor tosses his hammer and catches it a few times like a circus act. "I thought something that big was supposed to be stupid and have a brain the size of a pea. Instead, he seems as cunning as his disloyal father."

Elan nudges him lightly with her wing. *Jeez. You're a bit grumpy, aren't you?* She studies him with her head tilted to one side. *You poor thing. Is being stuck on the bank getting to you?*

Thor rewards her cheekiness with a scowl, his eyebrows lowering over his eyes like a red thundercloud.

Oh. Getting a bit touchy there, she teases before looking at me over her shoulder. *The small god must be feeling a bit inferior.*

Thor's broad chest rises and falls with several deep breaths before the red on his face diminishes. "I wouldn't get too sassy, young dragon. Although I normally see the fun side, today is not one of those days. I should be the one attacking the serpent, and you guys are out there risking your lives while I'm stuck on the bank."

Just then, Jormungandr flicks his tail and knocks Thor's backside, sending him flying for a few feet before he lands on his side.

Thor groans while watching the serpent head in the opposite direction. "I just can't get a lucky break with this serpent."

Elan's body shakes as she barely contains her chuckle. She moves next to Thor and lowers to her stomach. *Here you go. Climb on. Let's get this disruptive serpent that just swept you off your feet.* She grins, exposing her threatening array of teeth. *By the way, that was hilarious.*

Thor releases a deep, guttural growl as he hauls himself onto the saddle behind me. "You shouldn't be finding this funny, little girl. This serpent is very serious. He has been predicted to be my downfall, and I am the one who is supposed to tame him or fight him and stop him from causing Ragnarok. This is no laughing matter." He sits rigidly behind me. "If it weren't for the prophecies, we wouldn't know Jormungandr is planning to attack Asgard. It's not like he can talk to us." He flicks his arm at the serpent in frustration.

All right. All right. I get it, Elan says. *Don't get your talons twisted.* She flicks her tail, thumping the shoreline as we watch the Midgard serpent's progress. Once Thor is secure in the saddle, Elan climbs to her feet and projects into the air. Despite the added weight, she still manages to keep up. Her efforts are slightly more labored, her maneuvers marginally slower. Thor's stocky weight is much heavier than the lean forms of the Valkyries.

We spot the serpent, and Elan catches his attention by lowering then flying toward the Yggdrasil as though to lead him out of the realm. Rippling water catches my attention, and the serpent's big, beady eyes rise to the surface like he's stalking us. Thor catches sight of the black eyes and grabs his hammer, swinging behind us and aiming directly at the serpent's head.

The Midgard serpent ducks lower under the water before the hammer can connect with any part of his flesh then rises moments after the attack as though taunting Thor. His tongue tickles the surface as he exposes his long fangs, his eyes fixed on the god of thunder.

"That's not going to scare me," Thor yells at the serpent. "I've seen worse things than that."

As though encouraged, Jormungandr slowly weaves closer to us. Large murky scales along his upper body rise above the surface the faster he follows us.

The other dragons trail behind the serpent, swooping down and catching his scales between their talons, clawing the flesh and tearing wounds down his back. Jormungandr wails a high-pitched hiss and drops back. I squirm in my saddle, almost feeling the serpent's pain through the cry. With Thor's help, we manage to cloak ourselves in the dragon-scale cloak, and Elan turns invisible, lowering over the water.

Suddenly, Jormungandr arches up, rising tall over the water before flipping onto his back, soaking Thor and me with a large splash. The serpent thrashes and drops low into the water's protection as the trailing dragons keep an eye on the ripples left on the water's surface, swooping to attack every time his scales rise above the water. Without warning, Jormungandr flips and rises with his mouth wide, aiming straight for Naga.

Chapter Two

Naga swerves, flinging Eir to the side, her long light-brown hair whipping wildly in the wind. Eir stiffens and sits straight just as Jormungandr's mouth fills the Valkyrie's vacated space. The serpent falls with gravity and disappears into the safety of the water.

Phew! That was close. That had Naga scared. Are you all right, Eir? Naga projects his voice to all, probably too panicked to hone his voice projection.

Elan pushes higher into the sky with both Thor and me on her back. *I'd have to agree with Naga. That attack had me on my talons, and there was nothing I could do to stop it.* She weaves back and forth while catching the fresh breeze as she changes direction. Thor grips my cloak with all his might as though afraid he might fall.

The wind whistles in my ears as we fly, and the

thrumming switches from one side to the other as Elan twists again. When we're near the other dragons, I search the water for the murky scales. It's hard to believe a creature as massive as this can hide simply because of the perfect camouflage his scales provide. The brownish green of his scales allows him to hide in deep and shallow water. His intelligence also keeps him under the water, with only an occasional ripple giving away his approximate location. Every time we focus on the moving area, we find it's only seconds before the next surge happens many yards away.

The rocky mountains of Svartalfheim wrap around us, capturing the lake within their belly of the mountain ridge. The borders probably aid to keep the Midgard serpent within the water instead of slithering all over the ground. Although if Jormungandr knows he's in the wrong realm, he won't remain. The serpent may not remember Asgard. He last visited as a child, and the trip was probably not long enough for him to remember what Asgard looks like. He would have to remember that the jagged landscape of Asgard lacks the foliage of Svartalfheim. The only slight similarities are the harsh mountainsides, yet even these differ. The land of the dwarves holds dull-gray stones, whereas Asgard has more of a marble appearance.

Judging by the ripples in the water, the serpent is circling. Either he's lost or he's looking to cause more trouble. One thing is for sure—he's interested in the dragons. The four dragons soar in wide circles over the water, watching for the serpent, but as soon as he comes to the surface, it seems to ripple underneath as though he's avoiding the dragons' attacks.

I don't know about you, but I'm getting tired. We've hardly stopped for days. Elan's admission sieves away the adrenaline, drawing my hidden exhaustion to the surface. My muscles suddenly weaken with fatigue, as though bringing it to my attention accentuated the symptoms.

I stifle a yawn with my hand. "Perhaps you should rest on the bank. Your eyes and ears are sensitive enough to keep an eye on the water from there."

We'll take turns. Tanda's voice enters my head and likely everyone else's as well. *I'll go first—*

With me. Drogon finishes the sentence for her. *Tanda and I can watch over the serpent's actions while you and Naga rest. Get some sleep, if you can.*

Pulling my dragon-scale cloak away from my head turns it visible. I look at Hildr and Britta, and they nod.

Tanda loops around us. *Don't worry about our riders. Both of them are still with it. The rest of you, see if*

13

you can get some rest. We will wake you if something happens and you've fallen asleep.

Pfft! Elan turns visible and heads for the bank. *I doubt I'll get any sleep, although some rest would be nice.*

Naga lands next to her. Exhaustion mars Eir's peaceful face, and black rings shadow her eyes.

Dismounting Elan, Thor grumbles. "I've only just got out there, and now I'm back on the bank again."

Elan exposes her teeth, looking more dangerous than friendly. *If you weren't such a great heavy oaf, it wouldn't be such a problem. Some of us work harder than others and need rest.*

The god crosses his arms over his chest, finds the biggest boulder on the bank, and sits down facing the water. "If you're going to be a crybaby about it, you should get a baby nap in. I'm going to watch the other dragons and the water to keep an eye out for Jormungandr. I can't afford to let him get to Asgard."

As we rest on the rocky shore of the banks of Svartalfheim, it takes me back to our last visit when we were desperately searching for the expert black-smith dwarves to craft us a tether, strong enough to keep Fenrir secured.

The earth underneath my backside rumbles, stirring up memories. Visions flash before me of the times we were trapped inside the cave with all the rocks falling around us. We had to protect ourselves

14

from being clopped on the head, and it was all thanks to Nidhogg grinding at the roots of Yggdrasil, trying to punish the eagle at the very top. Judging from the shaking, the wyvern hasn't learned and is still getting insulted by the eagle and not understanding that Ratatoskr plays on the displeasure he brings. After meeting the kind-hearted wyvern in Niflheim, it's hard to be angry at him. Our meeting confirmed that the wyvern isn't exactly quick with intelligence, and despite the destruction he causes, he means well. He helped us when we were in Niflheim. Still, I wish he would listen and understand that the eagle's insults are not as bad as he makes out and he can easily ignore them.

The rumbling subsides, and I lean against Elan, studying the blueness of the sky. I inhale the fresh air tainted with the smell of moist soil. We haven't had much rest since we started this trek to save Asgard. We are bone-weary and fatigued, mentally and phys-ically. These things are firing up our nerves, making us irritable. That's probably another reason Thor and Elan have resorted to arguing more. Their friendly taunting is growing more personal.

Sitting forward, I crane my neck to see the god of thunder. The thought of Elan having to carry him reminds me, and I ask, "What happened to the ship you had at Midgard, Thor? The one you could fold up and unfold, and it turned into a big ship."

Thor sits straight and takes his elbows off his knees, twisting to look over his shoulder. "I gave it back to Freyr the last time we saw him on Alfheim. It belongs to him, and he only lent it to me." He scratches a patch of red hair at the back of his head. "It is a shame. The ship would have been useful today. Now that we're chasing the Midgard serpent again, we'll probably need it shortly."

I rest my head against Elan's scales. "We'll have to try and get it again, especially if we end up in Alfheim."

"If I had known, I could have arranged Eir to pick it up when she was there." Thor brushes dirt off his sleeve then turns back to face the river, watching the dragons and studying the water. Tanda flies low over the river, and my whole body tenses up to my back and shoulders. Perhaps I'm too much like a mother hen, but she seems too close to the water for me to be comfortable.

Eir pushes off Naga's side and strides to the edge of the water. "Ah. I think Tanda and Britta are too close to the water. They need to move up."

Naga straightens his neck and studies the situation in the water. *Naga will tell them. Naga worried too.*

Naga knows how quick the serpent can be. Concern fills the blue dragon's big eyes as he searches the water.

Before Naga can speak, Jormungandr's large brown head shoots from the water like a tall chimney. Water cascades from his sides, dropping back into the lake as the serpent aims directly for Tanda and Britta.

Chapter Three

Naga's scream fills our minds. *Tanda, move! Look out!*

The warning is too late. Tanda works her wings feverishly, using every bit of strength and speed to escape, trying desperately to go up and to the side.

Thor jumps to his feet and pegs Mjollnir at Jormungandr, his aim true. I clamp my mouth shut and hold my breath, unable to do anything as the scenario unfolds. Even Elan's eyes are wide with worry while watching the red dragon's attempt to save herself and her Valkyrie.

Thor's hammer wallops Jormungandr on one side, knocking the serpent forward into the water with a loud splash. He disappears beneath the surface again. The surges and disruption of the water are faster, more erratic, as though the hammer only angered the monster. Mjollnir skims the water then returns to Thor's beckoning hand.

After spotting the serpent's shift and the turbulent waves moving in the opposite direction, Tanda hovers higher. Appearing confident that she is out of reach, she catches her breath, and her gasps are audible through her mind speak. Her face wan, Britta keeps a tight grip around Tanda's reins. Her wide eyes scan for more trouble.

Elan climbs to her feet before lowering her torso. *I guess this is it. Climb on top, and let's go.* Before Thor has managed to climb on after me, Naga and Eir have flown off. Elan's and Naga's rest is over before it has even begun.

Our flight across the lake doesn't take long, but Jormungandr manages to stay ahead with his early start. The serpent's annoyance fuels his adrenalin.

Muttering to myself, I twist the reins around my hand. "Where is he going?"

I assume back to the Yggdrasil, Elan answers. *Back to the entrance where we came.*

My blood turns cold as I watch the serpent's waves betraying his increase in speed. If we don't hurry, we'll lose sight of him.

Thor stands on Elan's back and swings Mjollnir, letting it go to Jormungandr's foreseen location. The hammer seems to skim the surface then shoot straight back up and return to his hands. The ripples in the water stirred by the serpent fail to stop, even for an instant. I wonder if the hammer connected. Jormungandr is moving so fast, I fear we won't be able to catch up. Then the serpent slows a little, giving me a bit of hope that the dragons may catch up to him and hinder him from entering Asgard. All my hope shatters when I spot the Yggdrasil's hole just in front of the serpent's path. He may have been slowing so he would have a clean break through the hole.

Using my shoulders as his brace, Thor sits down. Elan's flight dips as his backside hits the saddle. "We have to stop him. We don't know where he's going to go next."

What he says is true. I know he's dreading the thought that the serpent is heading to Asgard to attack his father and all the gods there, yet I have no advice for him.

Elan increases her speed. *Can you stop it, Kara?*

How? I ask through our bond.

Elan grunts. *I don't know. Maybe with magic.* Her neck stiffens. *Perhaps you can block the entrance.*

I want to slap my palm on my forehead. It's so simple. *Of course. I have to try.*

Jormungandr approaches the Yggdrasil quickly, and Elan increases her speed, bringing us closer quickly. Magic buzzes in my fingertips, pooling in my hands, ready for use. Absentmindedly, I grab my blue stone necklace. A safety net of magic is stored in the stone if my magic burns out or I weaken quickly. I observe the size of the hole, mentally preparing the amount of magic needed to block it with an invisible barrier. I wrap the straps to the stirrups around my calf, hook my feet firmly into the stirrups, and release the reins, freeing my hands. Weaving an imaginary thread with my hands, I use the thread to blanket the hole, slowly pinning the sides to the edges, securing the magic in place over the hole. Hopefully, the barrier will block all of us, including the serpent, from leaving Svartalfheim.

The hole shrinks rapidly, although it's still too big to block the enormous serpent. Reducing the hole's size takes all of my concentration. The harder I work, the more I feel the drain on my energy. My body still needs rest to recharge to my total capacity, yet each part that closes raises my spirits, giving me more strength.

I work my palms in a circle, twirling the magic, imagining it covering the hole. The top edge is completely covered, and the rest is slowly closing. Jormungandr suddenly rears out of the water and dives, constricting his bones, and pushes through the small remaining gap and into the tree trunk.

Elan ejects a plume of fire. *Dragon scales! That was surprising. How did it get through that tiny hole?*

Thor shrugs then sighs woefully. "It has the bones of a reptile. It's fascinating how they can fit into tiny places, yet at the same time, quite daunting. They are very agile." He runs his hand through his straggly hair. "Good try, though."

My shoulders sag. Dropping my magic, I release the blockage over the hole as the enormous murky scaled tail disappears into the trunk.

Drogon and Tanda dive through the hole after the serpent as Elan and Naga hurry to the Yggdrasil to catch up with them.

He's gone. Tanda's voice sounds in my head.

We can't see him anywhere. Drogon seems annoyed. *How does that slimy thing get away so quickly?*

Thor groans, defeat ringing loud and clear. "We should go to Asgard and make sure he hasn't gone straight there. He may not have, but it's best to be safe."

The depression and forlornness in his voice fill my heart with sadness. He's usually positive and upbeat, especially when defeating our enemies. "We'll keep trying, Thor." I attempt to comfort him. "None of us are quitters." I tap his knee with reassurance. "Elan, can you please tell them to go to Asgard? Let them know we will be right behind them."

In a matter of moments, Naga is through the trunk hole, and Elan enters not far after him. When the darkness closes around us, the smell of wood is strong. As the passageway narrows, we climb the trunk of the Yggdrasil, swaying from side to side in time with Elan's rocking body. Rising over the lip of a new hole, we enter Asgard, a realm filled with mostly clear sky, marble mountains, and very few lakes. Drogon and Tanda wait for us under the shade of the World Tree. The dragons and their riders are searching the land before us. The serpent is nowhere in sight. A warm breeze brushes strands of hair over my shoulders and beats against my eardrums.

Thor calls over the wind thrumming in my ears. "Head to the castle. We should go alert my father."

"I can't wait for that one," I say sarcastically. "I wonder how he's going to pin the latest failure on me this time."

Chapter Four

T hor grips my waist tighter as Elan circles the
immediate area of the Yggdrasil, searching the
land for the large serpent. Drogon, Tanda, and Naga,
along with their riders, circle out farther. Our circles
become wider, doubling over what the other dragons
have already searched, just in case we missed something or somehow the serpent managed to blend into
the landscape. It's hard to imagine considering its
size, and his color wouldn't blend into the landscape
of Asgard as well as in other realms. Because of the
lack of rivers and lakes, he has even fewer places to
hide.

We search for a least an hour before being confident we've covered enough land to catch up with the
serpent if he was on Asgard.

"He mustn't be here yet," Thor yells from behind
me, attempting to fight against the wind blowing
onto his face and pushing his words backward. "We

should stop searching and head to the palace. I need to report to my father."

I suppress a groan and straighten my shoulders, steeling my reserve as Elan turns toward the castle without my instruction. She informs the others what we are doing, and the other dragons quit their searching and follow us to the castle.

When we land in the courtyard, Birger and Gorm stand at attention, and Thor takes the palace stairs two at a time. Gorm salutes, clicks his heels together, and juts out his prominent clefted chin. "Your father is in the hall, Thor."

Thor slaps him on the shoulders as he passes. "Thanks, Gorm. I hope he's in a good mood."

Birger's helmet strap slips over his chin. "I'm afraid he doesn't have too many good moods these days, Thor." He scratches his large nose. "With everything that has happened, he's often in a rather foul mood."

Thor grimaces. "Always good to know what I'm about to step into."

We make our way through the marble corridors toward Odin's hall. Den, the guard to the large hall, shifts aside immediately when we reach the ornately carved double wooden doors, letting Thor's caravan through into the marble room equipped with tall pillars. A small crowd gathers along the back of the hall, and a man kneels in front of the leader of the gods. His face portrays his distress over the outcome of his sentence.

Odin waves a dismissive hand at the crowd and glowers at the kneeling man. "Leave us. I will speak to my son."

Without argument, the crowd files out, leaving our little group of Valkyries, Zildryss, and Thor alone with the king of the gods and his wife.

Frigg sits on her smaller throne beside Odin's large one. Her face is pale, and although her youth and beauty are still there, her expression remains strained with the stress of losing her son. Dark circles shadow her eyes, and her back is arched as though her soul is defeated.

Odin sits with both arms resting on his armrests. His fingers grip the ends, and his pallid face distorts with displeasure as he studies the five of us, with Zildryss wrapped around Eir's shoulders.

I'm surprised he's not glowering at me. His squinted eye focuses entirely on his son, allowing an occasional glance at each of the Valkyries. Still, I brace for the blame, as is usually his reaction every time something has failed.

The two ravens circle Odin's shoulders then settle on the back of his throne. A deep intensity shines out from Odin's one working eye, belaying his anger and disappointment. I've seen this look many times before. He wants things accomplished.

Squaring his shoulders, Thor marches toward the throne and stops a few feet from Odin. He inclines his head slightly. "Father."

I stand to Thor's right, and the four Valkyries flank us. None of us take our eyes off the king of the gods.

Odin's gray eyebrow raises briefly. "I thought I raised you better than this. I thought I taught you how to be more efficient. You have warriors to fight by your side, and I send you Valkyries, yet you still cannot achieve what I require." He slams his fist down on his armrest. "Where is Balder? Why has Hel not released him?"

Thor lifts his chin and crosses his hammer over his chest in a soft salute. "I assure you, Father, we are working as hard as we can to get him back. While we have been collecting the tears for his release, there have been other problems on the realms." He lowers his hammer to his side. "The warriors have been to Jotunheim and Svartalfheim and have collected every tear except one. A giantess named Thokk refuses to cry. The Valkyries joined the einherjar to see if they would have better luck convincing the giantess." Thor lowers his face, filled with regret. "Unfortunately, they had no luck either. The giantess refuses to cry, even with Idun offering her the fruit of youth and longevity."

Odin's face turns red. "That is fruit for the gods. She refused even such a rare offer?"

Thor shakes his head. "She mocked the idea instead."

Odin's ears flush, and he hit his fist on his armrest. "The insolence! You should take the einherjar to Jotunheim and slay this giantess."

Thor strokes his beard between his forefinger and thumb. "I don't think that's a good idea. With all due respect." He inclines his head as an afterthought.

Odin glowers. "Why not?"

My leader rubs his cheek. "Although Hel didn't say as much, I suspect that killing the beings that refused to shed a tear for Balder will go against her rules. Besides, she isn't the only one that won't shed a tear."

Odin stomps one of his feet on the ground. "I thought you said there was only one who wouldn't cry. Who else hasn't shed a tear?" He paces angrily in front of his throne and continues before Thor can answer. "Why hasn't everyone shed a tear for Balder? He is the most loved of all the gods."

Thor clears his throat. "Loki says he will shed a tear after the giantess does."

Odin waves a dismissive hand. "Kill him too."

Thor crosses his arms over his chest, his hammer still in his right hand. "I'm almost certain that won't work. We can't kill everyone who doesn't comply. We have to execute this properly—even though your instruction is tempting. We also believe he was the old woman who discovered Balder's weakness and guided Hodr's hand to throw the killing blow."

Odin flicks his burgundy cape behind him as he stomps over the marble floor. "All the more reason to kill him." When he notices that Thor isn't wavering, he says, "Then go back to Jotunheim and approach the giantess again. Maybe she will give in this time."

Thor shakes his head. "I've already sent the einherjar back, and they couldn't find Thokk. They say it's like she vanished."

Odin raises his voice. "Then go to Helheim and demand Hel release Balder. Her father is purposefully making it hard to fulfill the mission. Vanir! Thokk could even be him in one of his shapes." He clenches a fist and faces his son.

With his mouth agape, Thor argues, "But, Father, Hel said she won't release him until everyone has shed a tear. She isn't exactly a bargaining goddess."

Odin storms back to his throne and sits. "Then you must make her release him. Haven't I raised you to be one of the best warriors?"

"Well, yes," Thor says hesitantly. "But I don't

think it would be a good idea to threaten Hel on her own realm. It would only anger her and prod her to attack Asgard."

Odin hits the heel of his boot against the marble floor. "Then you must use whatever method is needed to make her see that she cannot hold him."

"But it's her realm." Thor protests. "I cannot make her do anything on her realm."

Frigg rises slowly to her feet. Her shoulders collapse in grief, and tears brim her eyes as she approaches Thor. Eyes filled with mourning, she places a palm on his rough, bearded cheek. "Please go back to her, Thor. Please attempt to get her to release Balder. It's my fault he is in there."

Thor's defense crumples under his stepmother's touch. "You cannot blame yourself. You can't protect him from everything. Goodness knows you tried, more than any other mother would've been able to."

"That is my gift, dear son. My gift should have been able to protect him. So please, please go back and beg for his release. Give her the tears that you and the einherjar have collected. It is so close to her request."

Thor places a palm on the back of her hand still cupping his cheek and slowly brings it down, wrapping her small, frail hand within his massive large ones. "I will do my best. I promise. You know I will. I have loved my half brother as much as any. If anyone deserves a second chance, it's him."

A tear trickles down her cheek, and she wipes it away on the back of her long sleeve from her beautiful off-white gown that drapes to the floor. "Thank you." She sucks in a quivering breath, slowly pulls her hand from his clasp, and walks back to her throne next to Odin's.

Thor's face twists in anguish as he watches his stepmother retreat to her throne. He turns to his father. "There is another pressing matter at hand."

Odin presses his spine against the back of his throne. His eye is wary as he studies Thor. "And what would that be?"

Thor adjusts his belt of strength and threads the handle of his hammer through it, securing it behind his waist. "Jormungandr has left Midgard and is a monster much bigger than you could ever imagine."

Odin lifts his chin and fiddles with the strap of his eyepatch. "I have seen this monster's size within my wisdom's eye. Do not tell me how big he is. This may be so, but you have the power of the hammer and your belt of strength and the assistance of Valkyries," he scoffs. "Plus their dragons. You should be able to defeat one monster."

"The monster is cunning. He has wisdom beyond other monsters. He bears a deviousness just like Loki, with a mind to execute his ideas. And to make matters worse, he has a sinister drive to attack. I'm afraid he's not as easy to capture as you may imagine."

Odin crosses his legs, his back rigid. "You must make it happen!"

"But, Father—"

Odin shuts Thor down with a glare.

Chapter Five

Observing Odin glare at Thor makes me cringe, yet I remain standing firmly by my leader's side, joined by my Valkyrie friends.

Thor pushes up the sleeve of his jerkin. "And what would you like me to do first, Father? Go and rescue Balder or tackle the Midgard serpent?"

Odin pushes back into his throne, deep lines of displeasure creasing his face. "I want you to do your job."

Frigg gently places a palm on Odin's forearm and rubs it.

It takes a few breaths before Odin calms slightly. "The blasted hound is growing stronger even though he is secured. He is causing mischief." His face flushes with frustration. "These children must be tamed." He stomps his foot.

I swallow the lump in my throat and speak up. "Great Odin."

He scowls at me in response. If he acted any other way, it would've shocked me.

"Does Fenrir still have the stick jarring his mouth open?"

"Of course he does," Odin snaps.

I clamp my teeth together and attempt to curb my tongue. "Then perhaps the stick should be taken out of his mouth. It might make him friendlier and less agitated."

"What are you? Stupid? We're not going to let a hound have his mouth free to chomp on whatever he wants, especially one of that size." Odin's voice is shrill.

Inclining my head, I grit my teeth in a desperate attempt not to backchat and move the discussion to continue with Thor.

"She has a point," Hildr says, only to receive a glower from Odin. "I'm just saying. I'd be pretty angry if someone jammed my mouth open too."

Odin's disapproval deepens, and Thor interrupts as though to save us from his father's wrath. "We will do as you ask, Father. But what is it that you want us to do first? We cannot do it all at once. You know that I attempt to do everything you require."

"If Jormungandr isn't in Asgard, then forget him for now. Frigg is beside herself over her son. We need to retrieve him from Helheim." He places a surprisingly gentle hand over Frigg's hand still resting on his arm.

"Then we shall go to Helheim." Thor inclines his head and is about to turn when Frigg calls, "Perhaps you can take Idun with you. Maybe she can help Hel. I hear the goddess is quite… ordinary." Her face distorts with displeasure.

Deep in thought, Thor pushes his mouth to one side. "She is different. Which I'm sure Father has told you." He glances at Odin.

Frigg clasps her hands in front of her. "Then perhaps Idun can help her. She might want to offer her something instead of the full amount of tears. Maybe youthfulness will help bring out the goddess's beauty."

The god of thunder looks uncertain. "I'm not sure how that will go. Her looks are unbalanced, and it may be impossible to make the skeletal half of her beautiful by Idun's standards. But I'm happy to give anything a go to get my brother back."

Frigg rises and waltzes over to the nearby door. She opens it and calls into the next room. "Idun! I would ask kindly that you go with Thor and his Valkyries to Helheim to see if you can offer your services to Hel if she isn't happy with their accomplishment. I need my Balder back."

Idun enters the room and curtsies to Frigg. "I

would love to help them, Your Grace. Of course I will go. You know how much I enjoy making the goddesses feel better about themselves."

Zildryss flies off Eir's shoulders, circles Idun, and lands on her neck, circling her shoulders. The goddess giggles. "Hello, Zildryss. I missed you, little guy." She scratches his chin, and he presses the soft part of his cheek up against her jaw and rubs against her skin. He twirls gracefully on her shoulders as she approaches us.

Thor inclines his head to Odin. "I'll get the einherjar to store the tears for Hel's easy access, and we'll head to Helheim."

Odin dismisses us with a flick of his hand, and we head for the dragons.

With a heavy heart, I turn to Hildr. "I feel like we should do something about the stick wedging Fenrir's mouth open. It seems cruel to leave him like that. I thought the gods would have removed it by now. How's the hound supposed to eat?"

Hildr clenches her fingers around the hilt of her sword as though ready for action. "I agree. We should do something to make him more comfortable. I'll help you if you want."

I turn to Thor. "Do you mind if we do that?"

The god digs his fingers through his bushy beard, his fingers getting stuck momentarily in the red strands. "He's going to be pretty feral. What do you propose to do?"

Hildr climbs onto Drogon's back.

I climb on top of Elan and call down to Thor, "I don't know." I worry my bottom lip. "The Valkyries and I will go over there and assess the situation. We'll work it out as we go along. I'm definitely not diving in to get the stick. I don't want to be eaten by Fenrir. I have enough trouble with his slippery brother." I loop my other foot in the stirrup. "We'll come back and get you when we're finished. It should give you time to arrange for the einherjar to secure the tears for Hel." I firmly clasp the reins as the dragons fly to the place where Fenrir is secured.

On the dragons' backs, it takes no time at all to fly to Fenrir's secure location. The dragons circle the area and land out of the hound's reach. Brown matted fur cloaks the enormous hound's hide. He bares his teeth, his jaw working against the restraint. His canines seem to be much bigger than before. He's grown enormous, even in the short amount of time since he's been captured. The hound struggles, muscles bulging as he pulls against his restraint. The magical lead holds by fragile threads. If it were normal material, it would have snapped by now, and I still question how long the magical line can withstand the pressure.

Fenrir thrashes from side to side, his angry eyes slitted and spittle drooling out the sides of his mouth, spreading large showers on us when he shakes his head. My cheeks turn clammy just watching him. He looks like a feral beast, scary and more temperamental than before. I can only imagine how frustrated he must be with his mouth pried open like that all the time. Eating, talking, or doing anything else would be challenging.

Tentatively, we climb off our dragons, and Britta approaches with her palms held out. "Fenrir, we're here to help. We cannot release you, but we would like to ease your discomfort."

Despite Britta sounding peaceful, Fenrir's thrashing doesn't ease. The hound's eyes are wild, radiating fury, and he lunges at Britta. The Valkyrie shifts back, maneuvering quickly. Tentatively, Britta moves closer and keeps her voice calm. "Please, Fenrir. We're just here to help."

Fenrir stands on all fours, his posture aggressive as he towers over Britta.

Chapter Six

Attempting to snap, the hound darts again at Britta before being jerked back by his lead.

Eir approaches Fenrir from the other side, her voice calm and sending peaceful magic at the belligerent beast. "Relax, Fenrir. We've come to help." She moves slowly toward him, continuing her relaxing chant. But still, the hound lunges at her, his massive jaw clamping down against the stick, with spittle dribbling out the sides.

Hildr climbs off Drogon and approaches me. "What are we going to do?"

My boots thud on the hard soil as I slide off Elan's back. "I've got an idea." I turn to Elan. "Can you distract him while I get to work trying to get rid of the stick? I'll see if I can break the stick jarring his mouth open."

Elan's mouth quirks to the side. *Sure. I'll be the bait.* She moves closer to the hound and towers over the top of him, but Fenrir is nothing to be ignored. He is still big enough to cause her damage. She edges closer again.

I hold up my hand and speak through our bond. *Just wait for my instruction before you move closer.* I whisper in Hildr's ear and tell her what I want her to do, and Hildr nods before we head in opposite directions.

Fenrir thrashes, his mouth angling from side to side, making it hard to do anything. I pull my thoughts inward and talk to Elan down our bond. *Ready?*

Her golden eyes fix on the thrashing hound. *Ah ha.*

Now, I say.

Elan jumps in front of Fenrir. *Hey, you!*

Fenrir spins, facing her front-on, his stance ready to pounce as he assesses her every move. He sizes her up as a formidable opponent, undeterred by his smaller physique. He is ferociously confident. The hound braces on all fours, ready to attack, growling and oozing saliva from his open mouth.

I nock an arrow then release it, aiming straight for the stick. The arrow gouges a hole in one side. Hildr shoots the other side a split second after me. Her arrow flies in my direction, narrowly missing me after it slices the other side of Fenrir's stick. The stick

snaps in half, slapping Fenrir's jaws together. The
hound's glaring eyes turn round. He's too shocked
by the sudden change to attack us.

Elan backs out of Fenrir's reach. The hound's
confused eyes turn to me, and for a moment, he lacks
the usual aggression. He surveys me, then Hildr.
Then understanding crosses his face as he observes
the bows in our hands.

I pick up Hildr's arrow and shove it into the
quiver on my back. "See, Fenrir? We told you we
were here to ease your discomfort. We're not your
enemy."

His surprising lack of aggression is short-lived
when Fenrir seems to remember that despite the fact
I've helped him, he still hates me. He snarls again,
and we retreat quickly, mount our dragons, and leave
the hound to deal with his anger. As we fly off, I look
back at Fenrir sadly, thinking of what he must be
going through and how confused he must be. Being
restrained like that must make him feel so alone. Still,
I feel slightly better knowing that he's no longer
agitated by that large stick jamming his mouth open.
It would be nice to have the time to reason with him.
But we have other problems.

We meet the others at the base of Yggdrasil and
prepare to leave Asgard and head to Helheim.

Thor looks concerned. "How did you do?"

Holding out a hand, I help Thor onto Elan's back. "We managed to ease his discomfort. Unfortunately, it didn't ease his temper toward me." I shrug. "At least I know I helped. Did you get to arrange the transfer of the tears?"

Thor nods. "The einherjar should be moving them as we speak. They were pretty happy to see Idun again."

My gaze travels to the goddess as Hildr helps her onto Drogon's saddle. Her pale-blue skirt is hitched up to her knees to give her legs enough room to spread over the large dragon. Her strawberry-blond hair is crafted into a loose braid, showing her beautiful pale skin.

"I'm not surprised," I say. "She's kind and beautiful."

The dragons head into the World Tree and dive immediately, dropping us down and sending my stomach into my throat. This time, they make sure we stop before we reach Niflheim and become stuck with all the evildoers again.

Elan hits the realm of Helheim, and the mist folds in around us. The hairs on the back of my neck prickle as I remember the three Norn sisters and how they kidnapped Britta. Despite the darkness, my eyes are peeled wide, searching to ensure they don't come looking for us again. We don't need another thing to deal with. At times, I think I hear chuckles in the distance bringing an eeriness with the darkness. Clasping tighter to Elan's reins, I hook my feet firmly into the stirrups. Flashes of the nightmare of our first time on Niflheim taunt me, and I have to remind myself that this is Helheim and is supposedly safer.

Knowing Thor is behind my back brings some comfort. I whisper, "I don't know about you, but this place gives me the creeps."

Slowly, the dragons trek toward the river of Gjoll, and the thought of facing Modgud again twists my stomach into turmoil.

That giantess better not try to steal my soul again, Elan says, *or yours. We went through enough last time.*

Reaching for the soft part of her flesh under her scale, I stroke her skin. "I agree, Elan. I'm not looking forward to this any more than you are. What she put us through left me feeling helpless."

Drogon slows and paces next to us. *Hildr and I promise to be good this time. We will not stir her up. I want to dig my horns into her lack of flesh, but I won't, only because I don't know if that'll do any good.*

Hildr looks down at her hands and fiddles with her fingertips. "We're sorry for what happened to you both last time. Our anger got the better of us, and you paid the price."

My mouth quirks with understanding. Still, I

don't want to go through the punishment again. "We did not know she would be like that. This time, I just hope she'll let us through without hindrance."

We reach the bank of the river, and while still on our dragons' backs, we peer into the water.

Elan snorts out steam. *Yup. It's just like before. The river is full of swords, and so is the sky. Nothing has changed. We're going to have to wait for the terrible woman.*

As if on cue, the glimmering golden of the bridge appears around the corner, and my nerves drive a wedge into my stomach.

Chapter Seven

Staring into Modgud's eyes, I remember how I didn't want to come back to Helheim and deal with this skeletal giantess. The thought alone sends shivers down my spine. The bridge swings around to face us, leaving me staring up at the giantess.

She stands on the edge, her frail form towering over us with her staff in hand and her sunken eyes peering down at us. "State who you are and why you are here. You are not dead." Her loud, clear voice is way more powerful than her frame suggests.

Thor approaches her first, tilting his chin down with utmost respect. "My dear goddess, Guardian of Helheim and Keeper of the Bridge, Gjallarbru. It is us, returning to inform Hel of our progress." He holds a hand to his chest. "It is I, Thor, the God of Thunder, and the Valkyries with their dragons." He indicates us with a wave of his arm. "We ask with the deepest respect that you allow us to cross to finish our business, and then we will be on our way out of Helheim."

The deeply sunken eyes travel over us one by one. Each of us cringes under the giantess's gaze. Finally, she's finishes staring at us and raises her bony chin. "You are minus one and plus another. You are not the same group."

Thor chuckles. "Yes. That's right. I forgot we had changed. We're minus Sleipnir, Loki's horse son and Hel's half-sibling, and we are plus Idun, the goddess. But, I promise, our intentions for our visit are the same. Idun hopes—"

Modgud holds up a hand, stopping Thor. "She will speak for herself, and I will judge her accordingly."

Idun steps forward, her face sweet and innocent. "I am Idun. I come in peace. I hope to travel with my companions to speak to Hel over Balder's demise."

The giantess scrutinizes her for a moment before she taps her staff on the bridge, sending Idun on her way. Modgud glares down at the rest of our group. "I remember last time your group caused trouble. I'm having second thoughts over allowing you to cross again."

Thor steeples his hands before pressing his palms together in a respectful notion. "With all due respect, Modgud. We have a couple who are quick to temper, and they have learned from that time not to do it again. Please allow us to pass so that we may converse with Hel and then be on our way."

My throat constricts, and I bite my tongue, anxious to see if she demands more of us to lose part of our souls before she grants us access. Both Elan's and my energy were depleted last time, making it difficult to get around and function properly. We didn't feel whole. When the giantess narrows her eyes on me again, I can't help but cringe.

Modgud lifts her nose. "I shall let you pass. I better not hear of any trouble caused by you. You must speak with Hel then get out of here as soon as possible. You're not dead and have no right to be here."

Thor repeats, "We promise to be on our best behavior."

Modgud taps her staff on the bridge, drawing us up and sending us on our way. When my feet touch the soil on the other side of the river, relief floods my body. That was the part I dreaded most, and we got through unscathed.

As soon as we're all on the bank, the bridge takes off with the giantess in the middle. Under Modgud's direction, it swings farther around the river, searching for the next beings wanting to cross into Helheim, leaving us in the darkness of the realm. It was nice to have some light from the bridge, although we're glad to leave behind the whistling swords cutting through the air.

Eir leads us up the bank and cups her hands together. She appears to be concentrating until something appears within her palms. She holds it out on her open palms as though to give it to someone, yet no one is there. Blinking, I clear my sight to see what is in her hand, but before I can make it out, a gravelly voice calls from the darkness.

"You remembered!" Red glowing eyes cut a path to Eir from above. Soft padding of footsteps descend the bank as Garm progresses into view. The hound looks as scruffy as last time as he sniffs the cake on Eir's hand before licking the Helcake off Eir's hands, devouring it in a moment. After her offering, Eir passes through Garm's pass, then the rest of us summon the cake and offer it to the hound.

I'm surprised he doesn't get sick with so many offerings from the large group. Garm moves aside and rolls his belly on the ground, looking content. "I like that I didn't even have to ask. You can all go through."

After passing through, we follow Balder's dull light, weaving our way through the mountains, past the disillusioned beings convinced that Helheim is a wonderful place. It amazes me how these people can live an unfulfilling afterlife yet still be happy. Having come through before, we know what to expect from the occupants of Helheim and to pursue our trek with a casual stride. Our path is without obstacles, and I only hope this is an omen that dealing with Hel about Balder's release will also be this easy. Hopefully, she won't be worried that we are missing a couple of tears. The einherjar have stored the tears safely, ready to be delivered to Hel or wherever she wants them. Maybe she wants them added to Urd's well. In that case, it would take an army of warriors to deliver them.

A strange smell surrounds us. There is no fresh air blowing across the realm, and the scent holds an unbecoming staleness. The people in Helheim make strange noises, sometimes convincing me they are being strangled, only to find they are often wandering around lost.

It takes us a while to pass over the realm and travel to Balder's light dimly glowing in the distance, giving our minds time to fill with negativity over the outcome. Despite being more comfortable in Helheim's surroundings, a nervousness travels with the group.

I study Idun; this is her first time here. Her beautiful eyes, the color of the sky in Vanaheim, are wide, full of surprise and astonishment. She twirls the loose, long strands of her hair nervously.

Her eyes connect with mine, and she whispers, "They all look rather happy." Her high-pitched voice gives away her surprise. "It's hard to comprehend. It's rather depressing walking through here. It's so dark and gloomy." She discreetly searches the area as though it's all a secret and she can't let anybody hear. "I would expect them all to be crumpled on the ground and crying. They can't even talk to their loved ones. It's all just so terrible." She looks at the ominously dark sky. "Where's all the brilliant sunshine of Vanaheim, or Asgard, or almost all the other realms? I hope I don't end up here." Her tone turns more distressed as she speaks.

Eir grasps Idun's hand and squeezes it. "It's no use worrying about things like that. You are a peaceful soul, just like me. I can tell. Just keep doing what you're doing, and you shouldn't end up here."

Idun screws up her nose. "I sure hope not. This is horrible. I don't think I could do it." She stares up at the dark sky again. "There's not a glimmer of light besides Balder in here. And to think if Balder leaves, it'll be even darker."

We round several more mountains, and Elan stops, blocking the path when she squats down. *Get on. I'll get you through this realm quicker, and then we can get out of here. We've already seen Helheim. We had to do it on foot because of Sleipnir. But this time, let's not.*

I smile. "You don't have to tell me twice." I climb up then reach down to help Thor.

Idun gets a ride on Drogon's back behind Hildr. Eir mounts Naga, with Zildryss and Britta on Tanda. We're happy to take to the sky now that we've passed the area of flying swords.

After a few beats of the dragons' wings, we cover a distance that would've taken us hours to travel by foot. We reach the spot where Balder's light is shining and stare down at the tiny island that holds Hel's throne. The dragons circle once and land at the bottom of the stairs. We dismount and look up. The dread I feel won't go away, especially when my eyes focus on the half-pretty and half-skeletal form of Hel.

Chapter Eight

S lowly, we trek up the stairs, Zildryss wrapped around Eir's shoulders. Each of us looks as nervous as the other yet tries to act like everything is normal. We glance at the dragons several times as though seeing them behind us gives us strength. We cautiously dodge the presents strewn across the stairs as if discarded by Hel.

Idun's soft shoe bumps one of the presents, and it topples down a step. Guilt flashes across her face. "What are all these gifts?"

Britta grabs Idun's arm and gently directs her away from another gift in her path. "These are offerings for Hel. It's from the occupants of Helheim, expressing their thankfulness for letting them live in this wonderful realm and for her looking after them." Britta indicates the pile at her feet—they are all crumpled and tipped over—and shakes her head. "As you can see, she appreciates their gifts."

"Honestly, I don't know why they bother." Hildr's voice seems too loud for the area.

Eir shushes her, holding a finger across her lips, and whispers, "We don't want to upset her any more. It may be that she is the only one allowed to damage them. Anyone else will feel her wrath."

Hildr grumbles, "I don't like our chances anyway. She doesn't look like one that will bend her agreement just to be kind."

"You never know," Eir whispers. "You can never tell by someone's looks. Sometimes the least satisfactory-looking people can be the most giving and kindest. And often, the ones who are the most beautiful can be selfish and uncaring." She casts a side glance at Idun. "Of course, I'm not talking about you."

Idun holds a hand over her heart. "Oh, I didn't think you were talking about me." She grabs Eir's forearm as though spreading gossip. "And I know how selfish some of the beautiful ones can be. Trust me. I've seen it." Her eyes turn to Hel's unmoving face above us, looking more daunting in her skeletal throne. "I just hope that I can be of help if all else fails."

We reach the last ten steps of the long staircase, and my battle-trained legs burn from the exertion. I'm surprised to see Balder sitting by Hel's side on a chair similar to Hel's skeletal throne. Hel adjusts the skirt of her long black dress to fall neatly over her knees and shifts as though to shield Balder. Much time has passed, yet the goddess still bears a protective, almost possessive posture over the god of light. Despite everything that has happened to him, Balder appears calm.

Thor spots him and calls out through pants, "Balder, my brother." Ignoring Hel's presence, my leader climbs up the stairs and wraps his arms around his brother, slapping him on the back. "Good to see you."

Balder's light seems to brighten as he returns Thor's embrace. "Good to see you too." Balder pulls back to look at Thor's face. "How's Mother?"

Thor runs a hand over the side of his head. "Oh, she's a mess. She really wants you back. She's beating herself up for missing the mistletoe when she made all things swear not to harm you."

Balder pulls back from the embrace. "She needs to get over it. Hel has been looking after me here. I'm not upset. I'm not mistreated. In fact, Hel tends to my every need. As she does with the rest of her realm, which is why she ends up with so many gifts." He sweeps an arm casually at the gifts scattered over the stairs.

Thor slaps him affectionately on the back. "In any

case, Mother wants you back, and Father has commanded me to do so."

The Valkyries move up another step, and Hel holds up a hand at them and indicates for Thor to return to the steps. "Did you get them?" Her dark eyes are intense.

Thor stands next to us, pulling his shoulders back proudly. "We got all but one."

Britta clears her throat. "Actually two, but one really." A bashfulness crosses her face when she seems to realize she's not helping their cause. She continues quickly, "Because if that one cries, then Loki will cry too. Surely your father doesn't count." Her chuckle is nervous.

Hel lifts her chin and glares down over her nose. "My father also counts. I've noticed your insistence on one. Whether it be one or two, it doesn't matter. You haven't gathered them all, and that is what matters. This means you have failed to uphold your end of the bargain. Therefore, I'm not obligated to uphold mine." Her skeletal hand clasps her bony armrest on the chair.

Thor spread his arms in jest of helplessness. "But we are so close. Combined, we've traveled all the realms and gathered them, and you want to hold us back over one tear."

Hel's gaze turns cold. "As I said, one tear is as

good as all tears not delivered. That was the bargain, and you have not delivered."

Clasping his hands in a pleading position, Thor almost buckles into kneeling as he begs, "Please reconsider. My mother is beside herself. She needs her son back."

Hel's reserve remains unchanging. "I said no!"

Dropping his hands, Thor gapes, lost for words.

Idun weaves her way through us to stand by Thor's side. Her basket of red-skinned fruit dangles from her arm. "Perhaps I can offer you something that you may want."

Hel crosses her arms and presses back her back against the skeletal throne. She crosses her fleshy leg over the skeletal one and taps her boot on the ground with timed clinks. "Oh, and what would that be?" When she crosses her arms, it almost looks like a challenge.

Idun puts on her most convincing, sweetest expression and casually paces in front of the throne at the same time, twirling her free hand as though tossing imaginary magical dust. "I have what all women want." She looks confident in her product. "I have this fruit." She withdraws one piece out of her basket and holds it up to Hel.

Hel crosses her bony arm over her fleshy one. "I'm not hungry."

The pretty goddess holds a hand over her heart and chuckles sweetly. "Oh. It's not really for food. This is the fruit of youth and longevity. Bringing you youth is like bringing you beauty, and of course, we all want long lives."

A cloud settles over Hel's fleshy side of her face, and a deep, menacing frown crowds over her fleshy eye. "I am a goddess. I already have a long life." Her words snap distinctly.

Idun looks puzzled. It's probably the first time a goddess has refused her offer. She paces for a few moments, then her face brightens as though she's realised Hel may understand the importance of the fruit. Idun tries again. "And what about the youth? You could be youthful for much longer, and it can bring out your hidden beauty."

Hel's hands, fleshy and skeletal, grasp the edges of her armrests. Her fleshy knuckles turn white as her grip tightens. The frown on her face turns dark, much more profound than before as she edges forward to glower directly down at Idun. "How dare you come here and offer me the equivalent of beauty? How dare you compare me to the rest of the worlds living off Yggdrasil? How dare you come anywhere near me with this offensive monstrosity? I left those worlds to escape from you lot who treat me as though I'm inferior because I'm different and don't have a pretty face." She cups her face mockingly with her hands as though to emphasize her features. "I have lived with your ridicule, your stares, your belittling." Her words are crisp and precise. "And I will no longer tolerate this, especially on my realm, where I rule."

The air sizzles with magic, and a dark, ominous feel suddenly surrounds us, different than the eeriness we felt in Niflheim's mist. This is downright scary and worse. I can feel it building. My knees quiver as the change incorporated by Hel unfolds.

- Chapter Nine -

The dark sky of Helheim whirls ominously above us, lowering as though to trap us. The darkness somehow snuffs out all remaining light and cuts us off from Balder. The air grows moist as the mist gathers and clumps, morphing into a heavy fog.

Idun's knees quiver, and her face pales as she forces her wide eyes onto Hel. "I'm so sorry. I didn't mean to insult you. Most of the time, the gods and goddesses yearn for what I have, desperate for my fruit. It's seen as a gift. Because of this, I assume that everyone would like the opportunity to eat my fruit. Using my fruit as a bargaining chip is natural for me, especially if it works toward something I want." Her words are rushed as she tries to explain.

Hel slowly rises to her feet and paces intimidatingly in front of us. The clouds of fog follow her. "I'm not like the other goddesses. I don't appreciate being treated like others." As she gestures to our group, the air around us seems to shift, energized with something sinister. "Coming to my realm with these beings tells me that you are Odin's puppet." She towers over Idun, the eyebrow over her fleshy eye lowering like a thundercloud. "I don't take kindly to anything from Odin, and I have no intentions of releasing his son without something that I want in exchange." She pivots, towering over Thor. "You have declared war with me."

Hel thrusts her hands to the sky. The wind whips around like a tornado, gathering momentum and collecting any debris, adding it to its force. The ground shakes, causing me to wonder if Nidhogg is gnawing at the roots of Yggdrasil. This random thought is quickly pushed away when the surrounding mountains distort and break apart, morphing into hideous monsters with rough exteriors.

My feet glue to the ground, and I am unsure how to react. It makes me wonder how many more of these mountains in Helheim are these monsters. The sudden change of appearance reminds me of the lava dragon on Muspelheim. Narrowing my focus, I study the creatures, flinching when glowing red eyes shine back at us in the dark. They have to be lava monsters. As they near, the rock exterior becomes clearer, confirming my assumption.

The monster closest to us bends, bracing its hands on its knees, and roars, exposing its lava-filled mouth. Eir covers her ears with her hands, dropping them to her sides when the monster stomps toward us with ground-shaking steps.

A movement catches my eye, and I find strange-looking creatures clawing their way out of the ground. When released from their earthy graves, the creatures stand about the same height as a man. Decaying flesh covers the creatures' bones, barely visible as Hel allows in tendrils of Balder's dim light. The breeze carries the smell of rotting flesh while more of these unsightly creatures growl with strange noises, seemingly intent on causing us harm.

Hildr nudges me with her elbow. "There goes the idea that Helheim isn't such a bad place after all."

Without taking my eyes off the approaching beasts, I nod. "Thankfully, these aren't as tall as the lava monsters or giants, yet they're still too tall for my liking and too many."

The creatures shaped in the form of humans straighten their backs and waste no time heading in our direction. They advance almost in unison, releasing strange, twisted sounds as though passing through decaying voice boxes.

Hildr grasps the hilt of her sword. The metal

squeals as she retrieves it from its sheath, almost drowned by the thundering footsteps.

Thor laughs nervously, and he plasters on a friendly smile as he addresses the goddess of the underworld. "Please, Hel. We do not want any trouble. We came with good intentions, and none of us meant to belittle you. Our only intention was to hope that we could offer you something else you may want instead of the two missing tears." He spread his arms wide in an open gesture. "My brother means a lot to Asgard and to me, and seeing we were unable to gather all the voluntary tears, the offer of Idun's fruit was our attempt to hopefully return with my brother anyway. That is all. I can now see that was a mistake."

Hel glowers. "Yes, it was a mistake. You should never have come without bringing what we had bargained. We had agreed upon the tears of all beings who can cry only, and you have not delivered on our agreement. Then you come here and insult me over my looks and my life expectancy."

With eyes flashing to the sides, assessing the approaching monsters, Thor inclines his head. "I sincerely apologize. It was not our intention. We will leave now."

The thundering footsteps grow louder, and Thor's hand grasps his hammer as he fights the urge to use it. The monstrous beings are closing in on us. The decaying flesh of the mangled faces grows clearer, deeming them more unsettling than they were before. Their teeth show through their dying flesh, and the stench intensifies. The vision mixed with the scent drives me to fight my gag reflex and brings with it flashbacks of our time in Niflheim.

Elegantly, Hel waves her fleshy hand, then her skeletal one, to the approaching monsters and decaying men. "These are some of the monsters that I control." She indicates the large monsters. "The lava monsters from Muspelheim." She turns her head to the smaller figures. "And the draugar, the undead. Their spirits remain with their bodies formed by decomposing flesh and bone. They live in a world of pain and thrive on taking out their frustrations on someone else. I keep them buried for times like these." A sinister split smile crosses her face, one fleshy and one skeletal. "My pets will escort you out of here." Her eyes narrow on Thor before passing over the rest of us. "Never will you be accepted to roam my realm again. Don't even bother to try. Modgud won't let you pass over her bridge into Helheim. And I don't care how much you bribe Garm with Helcake. You will not be allowed in." She crosses her arms over her chest. "You lot disgust to me. I hate the way you treat me, and you will pay. All of Asgard will pay for your mistakes."

Thor stutters, showing a lack of confidence I have never seen from him before. "B-but you said that you weren't worried about Asgard because you know that your father can shapeshift and escape. You said you weren't upset that we had captured him." He ran a hand through his shoulder-length auburn hair. "What has changed? What has upset you and made you change your mind?"

Hel's tall form stands a few steps higher and towers over us. She places her skeletal hand on her hip. "Are you stupid or deaf? I told you this attack is because of you. You have fuelled my fire of hatred for your kind. You were disloyal to our agreement. Once again, confirming my suspicions not to trust you. You and your kind are conniving and deceptive." She turns abruptly and whips the long black skirt of her dress around her body, her feet stomping as she paces. "I will not be releasing your brother. I will be attacking Asgard instead." She sweeps a hand in the direction of her monsters and undead, hovering just out of reach, just inside the fog enclosure, as though waiting for her confirmation to attack. One of them on the left shifts closer, catching my attention until spindly bony fingers wrap around my arm. A shriek sends tingles of anticipation through my ears.

I turn to find the undead gripping Idun, dragging the goddess backward with unimaginable strength. Idun's long blond hair covers the goddess's distressed face, and the basket of her extraordinary fruit sways wildly at her side.

Hildr wields her sword in one swift motion, slashing across the mutilated arms securing Idun and the one securing my wrist. The hands fall to the ground, releasing their grasps on both the goddess myself, and an unearthly cry fills the air.

Idun jerks away from the monster, her face white and her blue eyes wild. "What is that? Why is it grabbing me?" She swipes her hands down her arms as if to brush off its touch.

Britta grunts and spins, brandishing her sword at a monster that grabbed her shoulders, only to find another one lurking behind it, reaching for her.

Hel's laugh is freaky and high-pitched. "These draugar are my pets, and I've trained them well. They will come after you, pursuing you even on Asgard." She throws back her head and laughs at the sky before narrowing her eyes on us. "In my eyes, you have committed a cardinal sin, and you shall be punished." Her voice raises. "I will be sending all the monsters of the under realms after you. They shall invade Asgard, and you and all of your selfish, conceited gods shall pay."

More draugar surround us, and a couple seize Britta. A streak of red flashes up the stairs. Tanda knocks them aside with a swing of her backside, flicking many away with her tail before sweeping her rider up with her wings. The red dragon stands on guard as Britta scales her wings and saddles her back, then the dragon takes to the sky, dodging the giant lava monsters.

Balder breaks through the fog, standing on one side of Hel, as if unable to decide what to do next. Torment covers his face. The god must contemplate how the rest of his existence will play out under Hel's reign if he aids us. This is now his home, and he must abide by the rules.

The clunking of gifts scattering on the stairs breaks through the fog as Drogon scurries up to Hildr, securing her and Idun protectively in his wings. Elan follows not far behind him. Hooking my foot into the stirrup, I launch myself onto Elan's saddle and pull Thor up after me. Naga darts between the larger dragons, levering Eir onto his back with his tail, Zildryss still on her shoulders. The dragons take to the sky as soon as their riders are securely on their backs.

Chapter Ten

Just as Naga pushes into the air, the enormous stony arm of a lava monster swoops down, barely missing the smaller blue dragon. Naga swerves to the side, flinging Eir from side to side with a white-knuckled grip on his reins. Zildryss is flicked off, and the tiny dragon circles around to land on Eir's shoulders again.

The hideous stone monster throws back its head and roars, exposing the internal bubbling lava. The monster swings its other fist, narrowly missing the blue dragon again. Naga labors to accelerate to take him out of the monster's reach and catch up with the other dragons. His big blue eyes are wider than normal, filled with shock and terror.

A strange gurgling bubbles up from the undead below as we fly in the direction we came, desperately trying to reach the Yggdrasil. Elan swoops as the hand of a lava monster reaches toward us. Her quick actions cause the arm to narrowly miss us as it waves up and over, nicking the tip of her golden tail. A strong sense of déjà vu hits me from our time in Muspelheim. The reminder has my heart thumping against my rib cage in terror, adding a beat to the song of the whirlwind that Hel whips into submission around us.

Summoning my magic, I throw a large blockade in front of the lava monster, but it seems useless to stop the colossal monstrosity. My throat turns dry as I watch it edge one foot through the barrier, followed shortly after by the other, pushing its way entirely through the blockade. I seek aid from the other Valkyries, only to see them far ahead. They are too far away to catch their eye. It would be advantageous if the battle maidens could speak with mind speak as the dragons can talk to us. Even if it's just long enough to drag their attention away from the lava monsters so we could communicate by gestures.

The monster below us rocks to its tiptoes and swings its massive arm toward us. Elan drops and swerves, and Thor only just manages to grab onto my stomach as he's thrown around in her saddle, his legs slipping off the side. The vibrations of thunderous footsteps seem to ripple the air, and sympathy fills me for the beings on the ground of Helheim.

Through the darkness, I barely make out Hildr's wan face and her brown dragon as he swoops then swerves to avoid one of the lava monsters. Something must be done. Somehow, we need to combat these monsters.

I clench my teeth as I go through the motions with my friends' narrow escape. *Elan, can you tell the others that we need to work together and watch out for my instruction to create a united magic barrier?*

It only takes a moment for Elan to alert the others, and the Valkyries' eyes turn to me, ready for instructions. Reverting to our battle-maiden training, I signal, and our magic merges several feet in front of the lava monsters' path. My nerves fire during the few seconds' wait for the monsters to reach the barrier. Seeing the monsters struggling to approach closer, I expel a breath. The victory is short-lived, though, and my blood runs from my face as they push limbs through the blockade. I shouldn't be surprised seeing these are monsters controlled by Hel. Loki possesses powerful magic. I should assume his daughter also wields strong magic, most likely much stronger than ours.

Panic grips my heart as the monsters continue our way, forcing us to retreat again. All thoughts of redemption elude me. I rack my brain for a way to stop the monsters from following us to any other realm, especially Asgard. The amount of time our barrier held them back is hardly worth the effort. Yet I'm not going to give up.

After I prompt Elan, she tells the others to wait for my sign again, and we haul magic from the bottom of our supply to create a stronger unified barrier, which hinders the monsters' progress, giving the dragons a head start toward Yggdrasil. The gap between us and the monsters expands, and my confidence rises until suddenly, the monsters' limbs break through again.

I had hoped the barrier was stronger this time, seeing as we gathered every ounce from the bottom of our magic supply, but I was wrong. Within minutes, the darkness of Helheim seems to close in around us as the lava monsters break completely through the barrier.

We drop our barrier at my signal, and I work on mustering more magic for another attempt, including from the stone in my necklace. *Hurry, Elan!* I prompt as the monsters seem to reduce the distance between us.

I am. Can't you see I'm flying faster than the other dragons?

I face the front and frown when I see she isn't joking. *They don't appear to be getting any closer to the Gjoll river.*

Her escape from the monsters halts as soon as Elan catches up to the other dragons. She doesn't seem to be going anywhere, even though her wings are pumping fervently.

We've been in this spot for quite some time. What's wrong, Elan?

Her wings increase speed, and her voice sounds panicked. *I've hit a wall. All of the dragons can't seem to push through. It's like there's a barrier holding us back.*

Peering over her side, I see that this is the mountain ridge that Garm protects. *Perhaps we're supposed to land and offer Garm his cake to be able to get through to the other side.*

That's a strong possibility, although I didn't think Garm would be able to stop us flying over the top. Still, it's worth a try. Without wasting a second, she lowers, informing the other dragons of our theory.

Before the dragons have landed, each Valkyrie summons a Helcake for Garm. Before long, the Helhound's glowing eyes peer around the side of the mountain pass.

"What's going on?" Curiosity covers his dark-brown furry face as his glowing red eyes survey the approaching lava monsters.

Holding out my cake, I lower it near his snout. "I guess you could say that Hel isn't happy with us, and we need to leave quickly, please."

Garm drools and licks the cake. I push it forward, and he snatches it up. While chewing on the cake, the hound says, "Well, I don't care what she thinks. If you offer me cake, I'll let you through." He adds sheepishly, "But don't tell Hel that I said that."

I scoff. "Trust me. We won't. All we want to do is get out of here in one piece, especially since Hel has sent the lava monsters after us."

Garm stands to the side. "Then pass on through. I'll keep quiet over where you've gone, but don't loiter. I'm sure they will work it out."

Eir climbs off Naga and pets the hound's cheek. "Thank you, Garm. I'm sorry that you have to live here. You have a good heart. We hope you don't get into trouble for this." She hands him the cake.

We all hand Garm his cake one at a time, including the dragons. Again, I'm surprised that the hound doesn't put on extra pounds just from our group.

When we reach the bank of Gjoll, I frantically search for Modgud's bridge. It would be the first time I wished to see the eerie gatekeeper. But she's nowhere in sight. We all line the river, each face creased in a frown. I worry my lip, my eyes searching upstream for the glowing golden bridge.

Britta rocks on alternating legs. "I hope the bridge arrives shortly. The monsters are closing in."

Thor paces beside Elan, his face troubled, and he balls his fists by his side. "I can't believe she wouldn't let him go because of one tear." The clomping of his boots on the ground crescendos as his anger boils. He glances over his shoulder at the fast-approaching lava monsters. "It's so ridiculous! One tear, and she won't release him."

Idun places a hand on his shoulder. "It is ridiculous, but we will find a way. Or perhaps he will be happy there. As the others said, Hel is treating him well and has given him a spot by her side." She rubs his neck in a comforting circular motion. "He doesn't seem too distressed."

A deep roar sounds nearby, and the lava monsters are getting too close for comfort.

Frantic, I search again for the bridge, with no luck. I know how much damage these monsters can do. I experienced it in Muspelheim and on Asgard. I would hate for each of my friends to be subjected to this. The monsters caused severe damage to Elan and me, injuring us majorly. We were lucky to escape their realm.

Hildr throws her head back in frustration. "Where is that terrible giantess? That monstrosity of a being? I can't believe she hasn't come yet. I wouldn't be surprised if she's making us wait here and face the monsters."

The monsters continue to approach, and we find ourselves backed closer to the river, constantly checking for the bridge's guardian to arrive.

Chapter Eleven

"Where is she?" I ask, more to myself in the hope that she will magically appear. I've started to give up hope, thinking we should group and form another barrier. Our past efforts to slow down the monsters have been pitiful. Our attempts worked just as well as the time we tried to stop the swords from going through the water and allowing us to cross this river. We desperately need to cross. My energy is depleted, and I'm sure the other Valkyries feel the same. Still, I dredge up some effort from deep within, surging it to the surface. The tingling goes down through my arms and gathers in my fingertips, ready to be utilized.

Finally! I hear Elan's voice in my head.

I peer over my shoulder and see the golden shine of the bridge coming around the corner from far upstream. The bridge's progress is so slow, and it sets my nerves sizzling. We need to get out of here now, and Modgud's taking her slowest time about it. I don't know why I expected anything different from this skeletal giantess who has little regard for us or anybody who wants to pass. She only cares that we serve her purpose.

The bridge swings freely, and I'm still amazed that only one strand of hair secures it high above the water. There must be some serious magic in that one strand. Although after seeing Fenrir's restraint that the dwarves made, I shouldn't be surprised.

The Valkyries prepare to hold up another barrier, merging our magic and shooting it just in front of the monsters. The shield momentarily stops them from breaking through. However, the groaning and moaning sounds of the draugar grow louder as they approach, following the lava monsters.

Again, our barrier seems to stop the monsters from approaching only briefly before they push through our barrier and their thunderous footsteps attempt to pound through Garm's mountain ridge. My shoulders and neck are tight with tension, and a headache is growing in my temples.

The monsters stomp over Garm's range, pushing through Garm's barrier without providing him Helcake. I assume this is possible because they are part of Hel's protective range.

We try the barrier again. Each of the Valkyries has

sweat pouring off her forehead in an attempt to keep this united magic barrier up. It's hard not to wipe away the moisture, yet I don't want to risk losing my hold on the barrier.

Elan thumps her tail on the ground near me. *Dragon scales! She's finally here. I swear I've had a baby since I've seen that bridge come around the corner.*

Peering over my shoulder, I'm awash with relief. The golden arched bridge has finally pulled up and swings over the water. The entrances of the bridge align with the opposite sides of the river. All that we need to do is convince this giantess to clear our path so we can leave Helheim. I wipe away a long trickle of sweat dripping from my chin, and my magic falters. I fight to regain it before it lets the monsters through.

Wanting to get everyone moving, I call, "While we try and hold off these monsters with our barrier, you dragons go first and take Thor with you. It's the only thing we have to hold them off."

I catch sadness in Elan's big golden eyes. *But I don't want to leave you behind.*

Drogon claws at the ground, leaving long talon marks in the soil. *None of the dragons want to leave their riders behind.*

Tanda snorts out steam. *We are here to protect you, not the other way around.*

"Actually, we are here to protect each other," Hildr says. "I agree with Kara. You dragons go over first, and we will follow as soon as we can."

But—Tanda protests.

Britta holds up a finger. "As Kara said, you dragons go first. We're the ones with the magic holding up the lava monsters, and we're the only hope at the moment to keep them away."

Thor grabs Elan by her front leg and tugs. "Come on. Let's go!"

Elan glances down at his hand, a strange expression passing over her face. *And what do you expect that to do?*

When she doesn't move, he tugs again. "I'll go first. You dragons can come afterward."

Elan scoffs. *Are you going to pull me across the bridge?*

Thor's cheeks turn pink, and he has the decency to release her leg. "Well, you know that's not possible. I know I'm strong. But I can't lift you over the bridge." His expression turns sheepish. "It's just a mere friendly nudge to move along. Now, come on!" He glances over at the lava monster making progress through our barrier, and concern fills his face, especially when he looks at Elan.

Elan huffs. *Better watch out, god of drizzle. You're acting like you care for me.*

Thor feigns a laugh. "Let me remind you how untrue this is after we escape this danger."

The sizeable golden dragon nudges him with her snout, and he stumbles forward. *Go on then. We're right behind you.*

The sweat is now pouring down my face, distracting my concentration. I long to wipe it away with my sleeve. I glance over my shoulder to see Modgud taking her time coming to the edge of the bridge. Just looking at the slow steps the giantess takes is driving me crazy. Her speed is set at one foot length at a time in approximately the tempo of a long-swinging pendulum. The temptation to shoot a bolt of magic behind her to give her a kick is too strong. I only refrain because I know it will make things worse.

The giantess has a strange look on her face, possibly even amusement, although it's impossible to tell with the lack of flesh. She appears to be contemplating leaving us to suffer at the lava monsters' hands. I grit my teeth, longing to wipe off her sneer.

Hildr grunts and curses under her breath, instantly pulling my attention back to the barrier. One lava monster has managed to get a foot through and is slowly shuffling half a body through sideways. It's unbelievable. We are pumping every bit of magic we hold into this barrier.

Eir groans in frustration. "What are we going to do?"

Sucking in several deep breaths, I regain a level head to survey the situation. "Everyone gather their senses and try and focus on their magic. We're going to release the magic at the count of three, then build another barrier not far in front of these monsters. It's the best way to hold them back for now, at least until the dragons get over the bridge." Checking on the dragons' progress, I see Modgud has finally reached the edge of the bridge, and I listen with half an ear to what she's saying.

Making eye contact with the Valkyries, I ask, "Are you ready?"

Each one of them nods in return.

"Okay, now!" I call.

We all release the magic then regroup it only a couple of feet away from the closest approaching lava monster. The other lava monsters stumble forward a few steps, seemingly shocked that their barriers suddenly disappeared. Yet, they crash straight into the next barrier and begin the process again of trying to get through our magic.

Knowing that the monsters are secure for this second, I peer over my shoulder again, listening to Modgud's conversation. The guardian's pleased face is making me worried.

Thor stands below the giantess with his arms spread wide and palms up. "Modgud, my friend." He smiles sweetly, putting on some of his royal charm. "We long to pass. Let me introduce myself again. I am Thor, god of thunder. I wish to pass and leave Helheim in peace."

Modgud's deep-set eyes rise to look at the lava monsters. Her back is straight, and her staff is gripped firmly in her hand.

Thor waits to be let across, a sweet smile painted on his face, but I can see his tension shooting over his shoulders even through his jerkin.

The giantess takes her time surveying the lava monsters, and a smile creepier than all of Helheim rises on her dry, sucked-in lips, exposing her teeth, which are barely hanging onto the jawline.

Keeping his voice optimistic and cheerful, Thor asks, "Well, what do you say?"

The evil in her eyes deepens, and she turns, focussing on Thor. "I see you have annoyed Hel. And for this, you must pay. You should stay. It would make my day to see Hel deal with you."

Chapter Twelve

"What?" I cry, and the barrier falters a little from my distraction.

A lava monster manages to get a leg through and roars with success. I gather my strength and direct all of my magic back at the barrier, interlacing it with the magic of the others.

Modgud watches gleefully, and she shrugs her bony shoulders. "If you have aggravated Hel, you should pay the consequences."

Thor's hands almost seal together in a beg. "Perhaps we can make a plea or a bargain?"

Modgud tilts her head to one side, the smile gone. "Do you mean like the bargain that you must have made with Hel? I'm guessing that when you couldn't uphold your side of the agreement, you were rude to her and then you demanded her side to be upheld."

Thor laughs nervously. "What gives you that idea?"

The giantess's eyes gleam with mischief. "Because she is showing her wrath."

The frustrated roars of the lava monsters grow when they struggle to feed their limbs through the barrier.

Deep lines of worry crease Thor's forehead. "Please, Modgud. Let us cross the bridge. We weren't rude to Hel, I promise. If there's anything that we can give you, anything that we can help you with, we are happy to bargain if you give us passage." His face lightens with an idea. "Perhaps you want freedom from this bridge."

A deep scowl plasters over Modgud's face, and she looks peeved. "How dare you? I chose this position. This is *my* position, and I'm proud of it."

Thor backs away a couple of steps and holds up his hands in defeat. "I'm sorry. I didn't mean to offend you. I'm desperate for all of us to get away from here. We don't wish Hel any harm, and we wish to leave Helheim in peace."

Modgud straightens as if to leave. "There's nothing you can offer me that I want."

Idun softly nudges her way in front of Thor. She looks timid but desperate to try anything. "Perhaps I can help." She inclines her head. "But please, do not take offense. This isn't meant to be offending to you." She moves forward and holds up her basket for

Modgud to have a good look. "I offer this, only if it interests you. I offer youth and longevity. Many people, especially the gods and goddesses, long to look youthful and live a long life, and I can help you do that with this fruit. Would you be interested in this as a bargain? If I give you the fruit and you get your youth back, will you allow all of us to cross this bridge?"

Modgud's face turns hesitant.

Idun picks up on this and says, "I understand that you like this role and you would like to stay and guard this beautiful bridge. This fruit won't remove that from you. It will only make you look youthful while you are working."

Curiosity sparks in Modgud's face, and she bends over to study the fruit in Idun's basket.

Idun adds, "If you like what I offer you, you will be pleased to know that it will work in a matter of moments, and you will have your result before you have to commit to your part of the bargain with us."

Interest sparkles over the giantess's face.

Something tugs at the barrier, pulling my attention away, and I turn to see another lava monster has stuck its foot through the barrier and is slowly edging its way through. The tension in my shoulders is tightening, and my gut twists in worry because we don't have much room to maneuver. If they break through, we may not have enough space to create another barrier.

Despite the looming threat, Idun's face remains peaceful. She's giving the giantess plenty of time to consider her offer without any pressure and doing it with patience I'm not even sure Eir would be able to muster in the face of this threat.

The giantess's hand reaches tentatively for the fruit without grabbing one, her bony fingers twitching. "So you say these make me youthful? Even someone like me?" She pauses then retracts her hand slightly. "I must admit my looks come in handy to scare people. But to look young again will be fantastic." Her eyes are dreamy as she smiles at Idun. "Believe it or not, I was beautiful in my youth. Many giants wanted me."

I can't believe my ears. Modgud is interested in what Idun has to offer.

Idun reaches into the basket, pulls out a fruit, and holds it up to the giantess. "These haven't failed me in the past. What's the harm in trying?" She twirls the red-skinned fruit in her fingertips. "If you would like to look youthful, you may be truly pleased. Will you agree to let us through if it works? We want to leave Helheim and go back to our own realm."

Modgud's skeletal fingers wrap around the fruit

before twirling it over and over as she studies it. "It looks like an apple."

Idun chuckles. "Yes. Many people have said so, but it doesn't taste like one. That, I can guarantee."

A flash of skepticism passes over the giantess's face. "So if I eat this and it makes me youthful, then all you want is to leave?"

Idun nods.

Modgud holds up a bony finger. "But only if it makes me youthful."

"Yes. All we ask is to be let across this bridge so that we can return to our realm," Idun confirms.

Evil gleams in Modgud's eyes. "But if it doesn't, then you can stay here and face the wrath of Hel and her minions."

Thor stands next to Idun. "It's not the life or the option that we want, but we will have no choice. If that's what the bargain is, we will stick by that. I've never known Idun's fruit not to make somebody youthful. Perhaps it will help you and give you what you want."

Britta calls over her shoulder, her voice strained, "I hope for our sake that it does."

"What is the harm in trying?" Eir asks through pants, yet her voice is still patient. "There is no harm for you, and you don't miss out on anything."

A frustrated roar comes from the lava monsters,

and a shiver runs down my spine. I quietly wish for Modgud to agree to the deal and bite that fruit. She is our only option of escaping Helheim. The amount of time she takes to toss the fruit in her fingers has me yearning to chew my fingernails.

Naga thinks it'd be a good idea for you to try it. Naga has heard that many people like the fruit. It tastes delicious.

Modgud's paper-thin eyebrows rise, and she casts a curious look at the blue dragon. "Is that so? Now, if I must be honest, you would be the main one I would trust to tell me the truth." She casts Naga a meaningful look.

Naga promises that you will not be disappointed in the taste, even if it doesn't make you youthful again. But Naga thinks, what's the harm in trying?

Zildryss runs around Elan's horns, where he often sits like he's king of the dragons, and he flies up to Modgud. The giantess doesn't flinch away this time, remembering how the little lilac dragon likes to communicate. He touches up against the side of her neck, pressing his belly against her.

Modgud's eyes open wide. "Is that so, little guy?"

Zildryss looks at the giantess with his big eyes, and his tongue lashes from one eye to the other in his usual way when clearing his third eye. Looking into her eyes, he nods with earnestness.

Modgud exposes her sparse, rotting brown teeth in a smile. "Then let's give this a try, shall we?"

Even though the Valkyries are concentrating on holding the barrier to stop the lava monsters, we watch over our shoulders, silently pleading for this to work.

Chapter Thirteen

Slowly, Modgud takes a large bite, and the suspense has me on edge as the crunching fills the air. Her lips are so thin that I can hear the extraction of the fruit's juices. Finally, she devours the core and licks her fingertips.

As we wait with bated breath, it pains me that I have to keep an eye on the lava monsters. The pressure is building, and it feels like they are bouncing off our barrier, trying to find a weak spot, plus the strangled cries of the draugar grow.

After triple-checking that the monsters haven't broken through, I keep my arms in place and glance back over my shoulder. Modgud's face warps, and gradually, flesh grows on her face, rising on top of the bones and puffing, ironing out all the creases. The magic then works on her whole body, and it morphs with flesh, beautiful and toned. Her cheeks are full, her face well-proportioned, and her flesh soft and subtle. She is gorgeous, probably one of the prettiest giantesses I've seen. The result is astonishing. I never thought the fruit would have such a strong effect on somebody.

Modgud looks at one arm then the other, her fingers playing on the flesh of her long arms. They then feel up her torso through the tattered garment she wears. Now that her flesh has returned, I realize just how little her attire covers her body, and my cheeks flush. I divert my eyes and follow her fingers' progression as they feel her neck, jawline, cheeks, and eyes, eventually grabbing her full, floppy ears. Wonder fills her face, and a pleased expression turns her full lips into a smile, exposing her complete, straight set of white teeth.

Long luscious eyelashes frame eyes full of curiosity as she gazes down at her body. She stretches her tattered skirt wide and takes in her lengthy, toned legs through the frayed edges, slowly raising one leg at a time. Manicured toenails finish off the pale-fleshed feet. As she observes her legs, her hair changes from thin, straggly gray strands with lifeless ends into a lush golden veil down to her shoulders. Her elegant fingers reach up and twirl the strands.

There's a timid, almost scared look in her eyes as

she studies each of our faces, looking for confirmation. "Am I really seeing this?"

Britta nods. "You look beautiful."

Hildr looks dumbfounded. "If I hadn't seen it with my own eyes, I'd have no idea that you were a skeleton only moments before."

Eir giggles. "I know it's a stupid thing to say, but you do look beautiful. Your eyes are mesmerizing, and you have long, luscious golden-blond hair."

"And those eyelashes are to kill for," Britta finishes.

A look of pride and satisfaction fills the giantess's face. She gazes down at Zildryss as if looking for confirmation from him as well. The lilac dragon nods.

"This is what you showed me, isn't it?" Modgud asks the little dragon.

Zildryss nods enthusiastically.

Modgud casts another glance over the small crowd at the bank below the bridge, our expressions seemingly filling her with happiness. Her gaze stops on Eir. "I can tell by how you described me that you're all telling the truth. Also, by your open expression showing your shock that this has happened." A beautiful smile spreads across her face, and it almost takes my breath away. "As I agreed, I will let you pass." She taps her staff on the bridge several times, and we all get projected up onto the bridge one by one. As I go through, leaving the last few Valkyries behind, the giantess says, "I will still enjoy my job, but thanks to you, I can be happy with the way I look." She studies the worn, tattered fibers on her garment. "Although I do think I need a new gown." She chuckles warmly, making it difficult to believe that it is the same person, but I'm not going to ask questions. Enthusiastically, I take all the help we can get across the bridge. As Hildr, the last Valkyrie passes, we drop our barrier. Modgud's bridge shifts and disappears around the corner, taking its golden glow with it.

In wonder over how the giantess transformed, we take another brief look after the bridge. It is strange how the giantess had changed after simply being made to look young and beautiful again. It was nice to see how happy she was to be back to her beautiful self.

Eir pauses on the bank of the river. "Perhaps she will be nice to the next few people who want to come through."

"I don't know," Hildr says. "She says she loves her job, which I think implies that she probably loves being mean. We just got lucky because we had Idun."

Thor places a warm hand on Idun's shoulder. "Thank you for coming. Even though Hel lost her temper when you offered her the fruit, I'm sure that anger was already there and she used that as an excuse to blow up. She has probably been planning a war against Asgard for many years, and this was just her excuse to put it into action. Modgud, on the other hand, was keen to return to her youthful self and isn't interested in causing war only to guard her bridge. So she appreciated your gift. That means your travels with us today were worthwhile," Thor says. "Who would've known this was how it would work out? It's a shock to me." He shakes his head.

We head toward Yggdrasil, and we glance over our shoulders to have one last look back at Helheim after we've mounted our dragons and before we enter the tree trunk. The lava monsters stand at the edge of the Gjoll river. One places a foot into the sword-filled river then pauses. By the change of posture, I can imagine several swords piercing into the monster's foot. I grip Elan's reins tighter, hoping the river will stop the monsters.

Before long, though, the monster trudges deeper into the river. Approximately a third of the way across the river, its legs are submerged into the water. Several flashes of lava discolor the river as swords hit the stones holding its molten insides together, briefly severing a bright-red cut as it exposes its core. Yet the monster presses on.

Thor hooks his arms around my waist, ready for Elan to take flight. "Come on! Let's go! I'm not waiting for these to get through the river."

Elan dives into the World Tree and shoots us toward the top.

Chapter Fourteen

E lan shoots out of Yggdrasil, and Asgard's rocky plains stretch out before me. The sky is clear. The dry yet welcoming familiar air of my birth realm greets us. The other dragons and their riders exit the Yggdrasil behind us.

Thor clears his throat. "Why did we end up here, Elan?"

I figure that Idun had done enough and that she doesn't need to come with us as we search for Jormungandr. So, seeing you hadn't requested a specific realm in our rush to escape Helheim, I thought I would bring her back to Asgard, where she is needed.

Thor lets out a sigh of relief. "Good thinking, my friend. Good thinking. For a moment, I thought you had followed the serpent here. You gave me a small heart attack." He wipes his brow. "There's no reason to endanger Idun as well. Let's take her back to the palace, and then we must go and search for the serpent. I would hate to think of where he's ended up now."

The dragons take to the sky and fly across Asgard, heading for the palace, and we keep our eyes peeled on the surface, making sure that the serpent isn't in this area.

Purely for comfort after the trip we've had, I slip a hand under one of Elan's large scales. "Elan, can you please check with Idun if Odin's palace is where she wants to be dropped off?"

Comforting warmth stronger than usual seems to encase my hand, and I wonder if I'm imagining it. *Already done,* Elan says. *It's where she wants to go.*

The dragons glide down and land in the courtyard to the side of the palace entrance. Idun climbs off Drogon's back.

Remaining on Elan's back, Thor calls to her. "Thank you again for your help, Idun. We appreciate it greatly."

Then, the goddess sweeps her long hair over one shoulder. "It's my pleasure. I'm glad I could help. It's a shame we didn't get Balder, but at least I got you out of Helheim."

Hildr harrumphs. "I don't think she would have released Balder anyway. Although we tried, it was an impossible task. We all knew that. But we gave it a good go because we were desperate to get him back."

Britta shifts in her saddle. "It saddens me that this is so. I would've loved to see him back in Asgard."

Idun pushes her basket farther up her arm. "I agree. I'll go check in with Odin and let him know what's happened."

"Are you sure?" Thor asks. "He is quite stubborn and pigheaded about it."

A knowing smile lights Idun's face. "I figured if I tell him the bad news now, he'll have time to cool down before you get back to Asgard after your mission."

Thor looks genuinely grateful. "You're a gem."

She curtsies, pulling her blue dress out wide. "As Hildr said, it was an impossible task, and if your father honestly thinks you could pull it off and also get Balder back out of Hel's grasp, then he's deluded. Hel is one mighty goddess, and she will cause trouble if she wants to. We have seen that."

"Let's just hope that she doesn't send those lava monsters to Asgard through the World Tree," Thor says. "The last thing we need is for them to come here. Let's hope the water holds them off for now. And after what you did for Modgud, I can't see her letting the monsters over quickly. Although, she is under Hel's leadership, and maybe she will give way if Hel commands her to."

Idun waves and heads toward the palace doors. The dragons leap into the air. Leaving Asgard so soon saddens me, but we have to find Jormungandr. He could be causing havoc on any of the other realms. There's no use staying on Asgard—we haven't seen him or heard that he has invaded.

The dragons land by Yggdrasil before entering the trunk again.

Thor scratches his thigh, and his fingernails scrape noisily against the leather of his pants. "What realm do you think we should try next?"

Hildr pouts her lips and pushes them to one side. "Well, the serpent did seem to go up. So I'm guessing that he went to one of the above realms, which could mean Alfheim or Vanaheim."

"Then perhaps we should try Alfheim first," Thor says. "We can check on the elves and make sure they're all okay. There are lots of rivers on Alfheim, and I'd hate to think where this serpent would go."

Is everyone ready? Elan asks.

All the dragons and riders say yes in unison, and they prepare to head into the Yggdrasil trunk.

"Wait!" a high-pitched little voice calls.

I cringe at the nasally sound, and instantly, I search the branches.

"Wai—" The voice seems to run out of breath before finishing the word.

Confusion takes hold of me. There's a strange sound accompanying the voice. It sounds like Ratatoskr is being strangled. I wouldn't be surprised because of the way he takes pleasure in passing on insulting messages. "Wait!"

There's something else in his voice that I've never heard before. It sounds like he's exhausted.

I continue to search the branches of the World Tree then the ground, looking for any sign of the squirrel's red fur on the rocky ground. A strange clattering sound makes its way around from the other side of the trunk. I slide off Elan's back and stroll to the other side of the Yggdrasil, leaving the others behind.

The clunking sounds again and pulls my attention. Ratatoskr is trudging forward, dragging something behind him, which clatters on the rocks. It's some sort of suitcase. The flattish rectangular bag drags at a forty-five-degree angle, catching every peaked surface.

It feels mean, but I can't help smiling. It almost seems like payback without having to do anything. Even though there is something familiar about the case, I ask, "What are you dragging?"

The squirrel takes a few more steps and very

lethargically drags the bag behind him. Every muscle on his tiny frame appears to be aching with pain and exhaustion. Ratatoskr grunts. "It's my message from Freyr."

I blink rapidly, processing the lack of insult with his comment. He must be exhausted. I eye the case skeptically. "For whom?"

Ratatoskr moans. "For Thor."

A moment of sympathy passes over me as the messenger tugs at the case, moving it only a couple of inches. The compassion wipes away quickly when the black beady eyes sharpen on me, bringing with it the memory of all the turmoil from the pleasure he showed when bringing me insulting messages.

I tap my foot on the rocks a few times, huff, and cross my arms over my chest. "Then you can take it to him yourself." I turn to go to Elan.

"Aren't you going to help a little guy?"

I balk at the rudeness edging its way into his exhaustion and watch him drag the case a few more inches.

Not bothering to hide my disdain, I say, "Why should I help you? After all the insults and rudeness and all the pleasure you took in delivering messages like I'm banished, now you expect me to help you? You're going to have to convince me why I should."

Ratatoskr waves a lethargic paw at me. "Jeez! You're a bit touchy, aren't you?"

Scowling, I spin on my heel.

"Oh. Come on!" he calls. "Like I said, I'm just the messenger. Don't shoot the messenger." With a clunk, he pulls the case after me. "Each of those messages were passed on to you from Odin and whoever else sent them."

A different kind of thump calls to me, and I turn around to find him facedown on the ground, the case fallen on his legs. He groans and pushes the front of his body up to look at me. "I know it's my job, and I take pleasure in it." He shrugs and half grins. "What can I say? I'm one of the lucky ones who enjoy their work." He attempts to pull one of his legs out from under the case and fails. "I guess you could say this is my punishment." He tugs at his other leg, and it doesn't budge.

I nod at the case. "What is it?"

"I'm only allowed to tell the message to the intended." After yanking at his foot again without success, his body and voice fill with exhaustion and defeat. "Freyr says it's for Thor and Thor only. And I can't give it to anybody else."

Crossing my arms, I ask, "Does it come with an insult?"

The sheepish look on his face says it all. "What

kind of question is that? Every message has to come with an insult. It's my job."

He struggles again unsuccessfully with the case, and my heart melts a little beyond my control. As much as I want to, I can't even be nasty to Ratatoskr.

Chapter Fifteen

"Oh. Give it here!" I lift the case off Ratatoskr and grab it by the handle. After checking that the squirrel can get up, I carry it to the other side of Yggdrasil.

Ratatoskr scurries to catch up with me. "I can't believe a god would make me bring this stupid case all the way here." The squirrel stomps and kicks anything small that's in his road, including a couple of fallen branches of the World Tree. "I'm a messenger, not a carrier." He clenches his paws by his sides.

When we round the corner and he spots Thor, he throws his paws up in the air. "Ah. There you are." He huffs. "I've been looking for you everywhere, dragging the stupid thing around." He indicates the case in my hands. "I can't believe that Freyr made me carry this around. It's ridiculous!"

Thor studies the suitcase. "It may seem that way to you. I know it'll come in handy."

Ratatoskr crosses his arms over his white furry chest and wobbles his head. "If you knew that you needed it, you could've gotten it yourself, or at least made it easier for me to find you. I've had this heavy thing to carry around, and for the first time, I didn't have a clue where to find you. Every time I thought I had found you, you were gone already."

Thor looks amused. "I've been rather busy with other things."

Ratatoskr waves a paw at him. "Yeah, yeah. Always thinking you're more important than I am. Don't worry. I've heard it all before from you gods. You obnoxious lot!" He jams his tiny fists on his hips and glares his beady eyes up at Thor.

Elan rolls her eyes. *Wow! You're one to talk.*

Ratatoskr ignores her and remains focused on Thor. "Do you even know what it is?"

Thor chuckles. "I sure do. It's his ship that folds away into a case."

Ratatoskr throws his arms out to the side. "Well then. You will know what to do with it. Just in case you hadn't guessed, he sent it to you to help you find that stupid serpent."

Thor reaches for the case, and I hand it up to him. "It has come in handy in the past. It's nice of Freyr to send it."

Ratatoskr stands by Elan's side, staring up at

Thor. "He could have brought it himself. It's such a heavy thing for me to carry all this way."

Thor fiddles with the handle of the case. "So are we just carrying complaints this time over what you had to do and no insulting messages? Because if you have an insult, let's get it over with. We need to get going and find the serpent."

"Humph." Ratatoskr throws his fists on his hips again. "You know I don't carry anything without an insult in the message."

Impatience grows on Thor's face. "So hurry up and tell us. If we don't defeat the serpent, all of the Yggdrasil realms could be in trouble."

"Yeah, yeah." Ratatoskr circles his paw in boredom. "Always the savior of the day. Whatever." He rolls his eyes. This is his insult, actions and all. "Freyr says that even though you have big muscles"—he flexes his biceps and kisses them—"you can't attract all the ladies. You lack the finesse and sensuality and will forever have trouble, never being able to find the perfect woman."

Amusement lights Thor's eyes, and his lips quirk. "Does he not realize I already have a wife? And I'm pleased with my wife and her beautiful long golden hair, perfect body, and a heart of gold to go with it."

The squirrel nods. "Yeah. And he says that you'll

never get all the ladies." Ratatoskr's eyebrows wiggle.

Thor sighs audibly. "Well, you tell Freyr that I have one woman that I am happy with, and I'm not interested in all the *ladies*. He'll live a long lonely life going from woman to woman, while I'll grow old with the one and only."

The squirrel scoffs. "Pfft! Have you met other gods?"

"Is that a trick question?" Thor asks.

"No. But none of the gods stick to the same woman," Ratatoskr protests.

A softness moves over Thor's face, and he speaks calmly. "Then you must understand that I'm different and I'm extremely in love with my wife."

Ratatoskr sticks his fingers into his mouth and dry retches. "That's just sickening. But I'll pass it along." In a quick movement, he scurries to the tree trunk. "All right, my job's done."

My feet are stuck to the spot as the messenger hurries off. I'm shocked he didn't bring me an insult. That's never happened before. It's a nice change.

I mount Elan in front of Thor and prepare to leave Asgard.

Ratatoskr climbs up the tree, balks, and looks down at us in surprise. "The tree is shaking."

"It's probably because you've sent Nidhogg

another insulting message from the eagle," I say. "You don't realize the destruction that that causes."

He focuses his little black eyes on me and shakes his head. "I don't think it's Nidhogg. I haven't delivered any messages to him lately."

"It could be the Midgard serpent," Britta says.

Ratatoskr shakes his head. "Nope. It's not him. He's on Vanaheim."

"You could've told us that before," Hildr looks at him suspiciously. "How do you know?"

Still clinging onto the bark of the tree, Ratatoskr shrugs. "Freyr told me. That's the reason he wanted me to deliver the ship. After all, he is a Vanir, first and foremost."

My cheeks numb while I ponder his answer. I turn to Thor. "Do you think the shaking is the lava monsters or the draugar coming to get us?"

Thor rubs his fingers over his beard. "Possibly. But it could also be Jormungandr moving between the realms again. We have to get moving."

Fear paints Ratatoskr's face. "I'm out of here." He scurries into the hole, heading up.

Britta asks, "Are we going to take Freyr's advice and skip Alfheim and head straight to Vanaheim?"

When Thor nods, Eir looks disappointed that we're not going to Alfheim again.

Thor shifts Mjollnir into a more comfortable position behind his back. "Freyr has no reason to deceive us, leaving it the best action to take. Jormungandr went up, so we should try there first. But we have to hurry, either way. If the monsters are coming through Yggdrasil, then Asgard is probably in more trouble. We could be facing the enemy in both directions."

Yggdrasil's branches sway above us, and at this time, I can see the trunk shaking and the leaves rustling even though the air is still.

"Can the lava monsters come through the tree?" I ask.

Thor rubs his moustache. "I didn't think that Jormungandr could go through the tree. But now I've been proven wrong. I wouldn't leave anything to chance. I think anything is possible."

The ground shakes violently, and each of our faces turn pale.

"Come on. If it's the lava monsters coming, they could be a while squeezing through the trunk. We should have enough time to deal with Jormungandr. Then we are free to tackle any other threat coming our way."

Chapter Sixteen

Beautiful blue shining skies dotted with fluffy, glowing golden clouds distract us from our contrasting mood. Knowing what looms over our realms hangs heavy on our shoulders. It takes a while for the magic of Vanaheim to weave its serenity into our tension. The rolling green pasture, separated by towering, picturesque mountains with cascading waterfalls and long, flowing rivers, temporarily removes the tension in our shoulders. Vanaheim is as I remembered it. Everything seems to glow golden, including the crystal-clear water of the rivers reflecting the glow.

It becomes a fight to keep alert and on edge while being surrounded by nature's beauty. I have to remind myself that we have a job to do and the realms depend on us. The dragons and the Valkyries keep their eyes peeled for any sign of the murky scales of the serpent. Surely their dullness will stand out on a realm like Vanaheim.

A fresh breeze caused by Elan's speed whips through my hair. Its freshness keeps me alert with its clean smell, bringing a refreshing fragrance of leaves and water.

It's hard to imagine such a terrible creature coming to visit this realm and causing destruction. In reality, the serpent was too hideous for Midgard. In all Odin's wisdom, he mustn't have foreseen the monstrosity the serpent would grow into. Or perhaps he did and didn't care as long as it wasn't on Asgard. He probably decided to send them anywhere after he predicted Loki's children would be the instigators of Ragnarok.

The other dragons spread wide yet still close enough to see the others. This way, we can cover much ground in search of the serpent.

Thor and I drop and fall rhythmically. The beat of Elan's wings lulls us as we search the landscape and rivers below. We fly for quite some time, seeing no sign of the monster. Over each river, Elan turns invisible and moves closer to the water, giving us a deeper look into its contents. Still, we come up empty.

Movement on a plain not far from the river catches my attention. A strange creature grazes in the pasture. When I narrow my focus, I see it's the same type of creature that we saw last time Britta and I were here. It looks much like a stag from Midgard, except with only one horn sticking out of its forehead. A golden glow surrounds its white coat, and its horn shimmers with a pearl finish.

I point down to it.

Thor nods. "That's a unideer. They are exclusive to Vanaheim."

"They are beautiful," I say. "They seem lighter and more unique than the stags on Midgard."

"It's their magical qualities," Thor says.

"Are they related?"

Thor shrugs. "Possibly. Kind of like how the horse is related to Sleipnir. The deer doesn't have magical qualities, but unideer does. That one is a female."

"How can you tell?" I ask.

"It only has the one forehead horn," Thor says. "The male has antlers coming out of the side of his head also."

"What magic does the unideer do?" I ask.

"They are bringers of joy and happiness," Thor says.

"Do you think we can have a quick look? Do we have time? I'm inquisitive over what they're like up close," I say.

Thor nods. "We should be able to spare a few

minutes, seeing as we've probably searched half of the realm."

I jig in my seat. "You've made my day. I'm sure Eir would be absolutely stoked to come close to such an enchanting, magical creature."

Elan circles down far enough away, careful not to scare the creature. Her voice projects in my head. *Naga says that Eir is beyond excited.*

I grin. "I'm not surprised. *I'm* beyond excited."

He says she's jigging up and down in her saddle. It's making it hard for him to fly straight. Hmm. I guess that's just like you did, Elan says.

I chuckle and beam at the thought of Eir getting excited. I peer up at Naga and notice that he is wobbling a little. It makes me glad that I ride a bigger dragon.

Elan lands not far from the unideer, and I'm surprised to see that she doesn't take off. Instead, she stands her ground, watching us approach. We slide off the dragons and head toward her. She has bright eyes of the deepest blue, and the horn protruding out of her forehead seems to shimmer pearl, catching the different colors in the area. The long white body reflects a pale color as well.

When Naga finally lands, Eir dismounts him quickly, and she rushes toward the unideer, changing her pace halfway as though she's worried that she might spook it. Her excitement is clear, and her face twitches with the pressure of not messing this up. She peers at Thor over her shoulder. "Does it get frightened of people easily?"

Thor shakes his head. "I'm not completely sure, although I have heard that they are quite friendly. Take your time and see how it goes. It's a she, by the way."

Eir releases a tiny squeal then approaches the unideer slowly while reaching out her hand. "Hey, little lady. Do you mind if I come closer and pet you?"

The unideer drags her hoof several times, bringing the sound of scratching grass with it. She snorts and nods her head up and down quickly while looking at Eir.

With eyes full of wonder, she looks at Thor. "Is that a yes?"

Thor lifts one shoulder. "Why don't you ask it again to double-check?"

Eir focuses on the unideer and asks it the same question. "Is that a yes? Can I come closer and pet you?"

As she moves slowly forward, the unideer scratches the ground again, tearing up the grass beneath her hoofs, and nods her head up and down with quick, jerky movements. She then pushes off to the side and steadily approaches.

Eir's eyes are wide with excitement, and I can see her body quivering as we hold back, giving them some space. Her mouth is agape as the unideer comes right up to her. The Valkyrie waits patiently as the unideer sniffs her hand before she slowly strokes the creature's snout and head, scratching her behind the ears. The unideer bends in to her touch, holding still as she feels the animal's horn. Beams of rainbow light explode from the horn on the unideer's forehead and circle the air around them. A deeper peacefulness settles over Eir's face. At the same time, I can see she's having trouble holding back her excited squeal.

"Aren't you beautiful?" she coos to the creature. "I wish we had you on Asgard."

The unideer grunts softly and nods.

I turn back to the Elan's saddle, bring out two apples I know are stored in the saddlebag for our long trip, and slowly head back to the magical animal. Storing one inside my uniform, I hold the other out for Eir. "Perhaps you want to give her this?"

Appreciation fills Eir's eyes as she looks at the apple then at me. "No. I think you should give it to her."

My heart thumps with excitement. "Are you sure?"

"Of course." She nods to the unideer, and I approach slowly, watching as she snavels it up from my extended open palm.

Chapter Seventeen

While the unideer chews on the apple, I brush the side of her cheek, and she nudges into me. Even though I have seen her from a distance on our last visit, she's more impressive up close. I'm so fascinated by the unideer and the pearlized tinge to her white coat that a sound off to the side startles me. I hadn't noticed any dragons or any of my companions in that direction. Curious, I turn to see a white stag with a horn in the middle of his forehead like the unideer. He has a generous display of antlers crowning his head. He's as stunning and unique as the unideer.

My body gravitates toward the stag, pushed faster forward when the unideer nudges me with her nose. The added oomph causes me to stumble slightly. Stopping only a few feet away from the animal, I gaze back at the unideer. "Is this your partner?"

The unideer snorts and nudges me closer again. Grabbing the second apple that I'd stashed in my uniform, I hold it out for the stag. He sniffs the apple then bites off chunks as I hold it in my flat palm. Slowly, I run a hand over his pearlized snout. He's the same color as the unideer.

A flash of lilac glides around my head then lands on my shoulder. I cackle. "Hello, little guy. Have you come to have a look too?"

Zildryss runs down my arm and sits next to the apple. As the stag finishes his mouthful, he studies the little dragon then touches his nose to Zildryss's tiny one. The lilac dragon draws one long lick over the stag's pale-pink nose. The stag startles, his eyes going wide, and his movements pause before he licks the little dragon back with his long, broad tongue.

Zildryss chirrups with amusement and leaps up to the stag's antlers before swinging from their ends. He flips a few times, catching the wind beneath his little wings, then lands on my shoulder.

Aww! Naga thinks the stag likes the Zildryss.

Eir giggles. "I also think Zildryss likes the stag."

My smile broadens. "Two magical creatures playing together."

Britta moves closer, and the unideer allows her to pet her along her snout. "It's so lovely to see."

Suddenly, the ground rattles and shakes, and both

the stag and the unideer take off into the bushes, their galloping footprints fading. Eyes wide, we search the area before facing each other.

Britta grabs Tanda's reins. "Do you think that's the Midgard serpent?"

Hildr yanks herself onto Drogon's waiting back. "Either that or the lava monsters."

Following Hildr's lead, I climb onto Elan's back and hold out a hand to Thor. "I honestly hope it's neither. Let's check it out." I brace myself as I pull Thor onto the saddle.

Within seconds, Britta is on Tanda's back, and Naga almost lifts Eir with his nose onto his back. We take to the sky, searching for both Jormungandr and Hel's minions. We spread out to cover more land. Any of these monsters will be a stark contrast to the beautiful, peaceful backdrop of Vanaheim.

After an hour of searching, I catch sight of familiar territory that brings up uncomfortable memories. I tug at the sides of my cloak like it's a protective shield and point that way. "We should go and ask the fossegrim. Perhaps he has seen Jormungandr. After all, the water is his natural stomping ground."

Elan sets her sights on the fossegrim's lake. *Good thinking.*

Thor's hot breath warms my ear as he asks, "What is a fossegrim?"

I grunt, unamused. "A very sly creature. He lures young maidens into the river, giving them a watery death."

"Nice," Thor says sarcastically. "How does he do that?"

"He plays a fiddle, and the tune holds possessing magic. The women can't hear or think of anything other than the tune. They are so spellbound by his music that it tricks them into thinking they are deeply in love with him."

Thor whistles. "Wow! That's some deceptive power."

Elan scoffs. *You'll believe that more once you see him.*

"He's that bad, huh?" Thor asks.

Elan flies us through a fluffy cloud that momentarily obscures the land below. *I know my tastes are different, being a dragon, but I would bet you a cow that he is one ugly man.*

I nod. "She's got that right. Even so, we had to save Idun from his grasp."

Elan passes through another cloud, and precipitation covers us, dampening our exposed skin. *That was interesting. We had to let Britta be the bait and have her exposed to the music to follow where Idun went.* We exit the cloud, and Elan grins at Thor over her shoulder. *Once we found him, we threatened him.*

"How?" Thor asks.

"With very forceful persuasion, we made him promise not to leave his area to lure maidens purposefully," I say.

Thor adjusts his hammer's position. "Sounds like an interesting character and rather dangerous, seeing as we have all women around. Are you sure it's a good idea to take all of the Valkyries to him? From what you say, you'll only be fuelling his desire."

Opening the saddlebag, I pull out small pieces of cloth and squeeze them into earplugs. "We have that covered. Elan, please tell everyone to put plugs in their ears. We don't want a repeat of last time."

You got it!

The distance between the dragons closes, and each of the Valkyries finds something to use as earplugs. Britta is the first to comply, knowing precisely what to expect, while the others, looking puzzled, follow instructions.

Tanda leads the way to the fossegrim's lake and drops closer to the water. Elan follows suit, and Drogon and Naga catch up and trail behind.

Tanda circles, and I catch sight of her face. Her eyes glow a deep red while fixed on the little man, and her scales bunch together with disapproval. The fossegrim sits on his favorite rock, jutting out from the deep water like a tiny island, rapidly playing his fiddle. My anger rises as I study the squatting little man hunched over his bow and fiddle. I'm thankful for the earplugs. By the way he is playing and the speed that he's dragging that bow across the strings, I suspect he's playing at a volume well over the level we demanded.

Elan grabs my attention. *Kara, you're not going to like this. Have a good look over the other side.*

Cringing, I peer over Elan's enormous golden form, and she tilts her body, giving me an unobscured vision. Peering through the crystal clearness of the lake, I spot all the women in their watery graves surrounding the fossegrim's stone island. My eyes travel to the edge of the water, and I freeze. A young maiden wades off the bank, swaying deeper into the water toward the fiddler.

Thor yells into my plugged ear. "What is she doing?" His voice is muffled, but I'm barely able to understand him.

I shift into a slightly more comfortable position. "She doesn't know. That's the problem. She is acting as I tried to explain. It's much more disturbing seeing it in play. Believe it or not, she is fixated on the fossegrim, thinking that weasel's the most handsome man in the world, who will fulfill all her dreams. She won't be able to eat or sleep or leave his side until he stops playing his fiddle. Unbeknown to her, she's going to a watery death."

Thor growls. "That's terrible!"

"Yes, it is terrible. We tried to stop it. We have warning signs placed at the outskirts of his normal range, but he must be playing louder than normal. If he is, then he's not keeping the agreement. We didn't stop him from playing but demanded that when he plays, he keeps it quieter, so it stays within the boundary we had arranged so young maidens passing by wouldn't fall into his trap."

I glower at the fossegrim, whose eyes are set on the approaching maiden. "We were lured into the same outcome. If it weren't for Zildryss and the dragons that can't hear the music, that would have been us at the bottom of the lake." I point to the bodies under the water. "We also warned the nearby villages that reported several missing maidens over the years. Despite our efforts, it doesn't mean a young maiden won't be walking this way and miss all the signs, especially if the music reaches them before they see the warnings." I push the material plugs farther into my ears as we get closer. "The fossegrim's music may be so loud it captured this maiden before she reached the signs. Or he did the other thing we forbade. He played his fiddle near the path and lured the young woman from there to his lair."

Thor's mouth moves to say something, but I can't hear him now that my plugs are pushed in farther.

Just watch us. Elan says, and I assume she must be answering Thor's question. She swoops down and lands on the shoreline.

As an added measure, I cover my plugged ears with my palms. I turn to Thor. "It's best if you try and stop her. You're not susceptible to the music as he is not trying to lure a male."

Thor rapidly slides off Elan's back and charges to the waterline to aid the woman.

- Chapter Eighteen -

Thor yanks the woman's arm, hauling her from the water. She struggles against him, and it's surprising how much strength she musters.

Shock plasters over Thor's face, yet he braces his posture and lugs her toward the bank. She thrashes, splashing wildly as she jerks away from him. His grasp is tight as tosses her over his shoulder and plunks her halfway up the shoreline.

"What are you doing?" the woman cries. "Why are you dragging me away from my true love?" She kicks at Thor, her sodden skirt weighing her legs down. Thor clasps her wrist, and she slaps his hand. "Let me go! Unhand me!"

Bemused, Thor ignores her demands and pulls her farther up the bank, guarding her to make sure she stays out of the water.

After dismounting, I stand on the shoreline with

my hands on my hips. I watch the display before turning to the fossegrim.

Britta joins me and demands of the strange man, "What are you doing?"

The fossegrim stills his bow and turns his dark eyes on us. He grins, showing off his sparse teeth.

When he doesn't answer, I say, "The agreement was that you weren't to lure any more maidens."

The fossegrim lowers his fiddle, half hiding it behind his back. I dislodge one earplug, keeping the other in case I need to block them again quickly.

A scrawny shoulder of the fossegrim lifts into what looks like a shrug, and he flutters his eyelids, portraying innocence. "I was simply playing music. That is all I was doing."

I growl at his lack of remorse. "I should string you up upside down from the nearest tree and sink your fiddle into a spot you will never find."

Tanda towers protectively over Britta. *Or one of the dragons could smash your fiddle.*

Britta's eyes sparkle. "Now, there's an idea."

Drogon claws at the ground, leaving long talon tracks in the soil. *Here, let me.*

I would be happy to smash that fiddle too. Elan grins, exposing her fierce array of sharp teeth. The expression still has me looking twice to check that she's my friendly companion.

Hildr joins us by Drogon's side. "Do you hear that, fossegrim? We have many volunteers wanting to trash that fiddle of yours."

The scrawny man hugs the fiddle to his chest. "Not my precious fiddle."

Grunting, I wave a frustrated hand at him. "So why do you tempt its fate?"

The hunched figure shrugs with both shoulders, still grasping his precious instrument. "I was bored."

"In your boredom, did you happen to see Jormungandr, the Midgard serpent, travel through these waters?" I ask.

His lined face morphs with a frown. "What's the Midgard serpent?"

Britta tosses her head back with frustration. "Come on. You can't be that naïve."

His frown deepens. "You said Midgard serpent?" He strokes his chin. "If it's not from Vanaheim, I have no idea what it is."

Tanda growls, and the fossegrim clutches his legs, folding himself so tightly in a squatting position his knees touch his ears. The position reminds me of a turtle retracting into its shell.

The uncertainty in his eyes makes me give him the benefit of the doubt. "It is a large serpent, even bigger than the dragons, with murky brownish-green scales. You won't miss it if it comes through here."

His eyes light up, and he releases his legs. "Oh. Is that what you're talking about? Yes. I think I saw something like that not long ago."

I move closer to the water's edge. "Which way did he go?"

The fossegrim grins, and an eerie air shifts around me. "What's in it for me?"

Thor stomps down the bank. "Why you lit—"

Knowing Thor's anger won't get us anywhere, I grasp his arm to stop him.

A shadow passes over us, and I glance up to see Elan standing above us. "How about I don't eat your sorry butt."

Disappointment fills the fossegrim's face. "Are you going to be like that again?" He shakes his head. "All right then. You lot are no fun." He points to the farthest spot over his shoulder. "It went that way. I didn't interact with it. It's enormous."

"Do you know where he was going?" Thor asks.

The fossegrim shakes his head. "I was just happy it left my waters quickly and left me alone. I don't like being disrupted like that. I haven't thought about it again until now."

The young woman on the bank rises to her feet. With the music no longer playing, her sanity has returned, leaving her confused. "Where am I?"

Thor's face twists with disbelief. "Don't you know?"

Her wet ankle-length skirt wraps around her legs, making it difficult to walk. "No. I have no idea. Why am I near a river?"

"You were lured by this little man in the middle of the water," I say, gesturing to the fossegrim.

She pulls at her soaked clothes. "Why am I wet?"

Britta places a hand on her hip. "Again, the little man in the middle. He had you under his spell and lured you into the water."

Her jaw drops, and her feet falter. "Wha—"

Placing a hand on her shoulder, I say, "I recommend that you leave now and don't come near this area again unless you have earplugs in. His music is dangerous to all maidens. If you don't heed my warning, he will lead you to a watery grave."

She blinks a few times, trying to clear the shock, before scrambling off in the other direction. At times, she looks back, casting disgusted looks at the fossegrim.

I return to rebuke the fossegrim. "You're lucky you could give us some useful information this time, or I would have my dragon smash that fiddle of yours."

In a pitiful effort, he grabs his fiddle and tucks it

behind his back as though that could protect it from one of the leering dragons.

Turning to Eir and Naga, I ask, "Would you mind hanging back to check that the young woman escapes from the reach of the music?"

Naga frowns at the fossegrim. *Naga is happy to make sure the woman is safe. Naga is pleased for maidens to have mates, but this isn't right.*

Eir strokes his side and climbs on top. "Come on, Naga. Let's make sure the maiden has a chance to find a love mate."

Naga snorts at the little man on the rock then pushes into the sky, his light-blue wings with white stars underneath blending into the sky within moments.

We climb back onto our dragons and take to the sky. As we pass over the lake, Tanda swoops low, snapping her teeth threateningly at the fossegrim. The little man ducks, hiding his body between his knees so tight he is almost a ball balancing on the rock in the middle of the lake.

Drogon blows out a plume of fire. *Be thankful the Valkyries dealt you their justice. If I find you doing the same, this will be my justice with direct aim.* He expels a long plume of fire, skimming the top of the water slightly to the right of the little man.

Elan swings her tail and wacks it against the

water's surface, dousing the fossegrim with a wall of water before leaping into the sky with Thor and me on her back. The dragons head in the direction the fossegrim said the serpent went, eyes wide and searching for a glimpse of its scales.

After we've traveled a few minutes, I turn back and see that despite the dragon's threats, the fossegrim has his fiddle raised to his chin and his bow poised. I shove the second plug into my ear and tell Elan to warn the others. A surge of worry washes over me for the young maiden, only to be swept away when I see Naga in the far distance. She should be out of reach of the music's lure.

Thor gazes over his shoulder at the fossegrim. "I should've obliterated his chance to play his music. If the fight to save us from Ragnarok weren't so great, and we didn't need important information from him, I would deal him his correct justice."

Nodding, I say, "I know what you mean. I should have done something on our first visit, but this isn't my realm to deal justice. Besides, I'm just a Valkyrie, not a goddess."

I turn my full attention to the search for the serpent. In the worst case, we need to get him away from Vanaheim and back to Midgard and into lakes where he belongs.

Elan swerves from side to side, dodging between

the trees as we fly low over the river. Thor's fingers dig into my sides as we tilt. A quick look shows me that Drogon and Tanda are not far behind, with Naga closing the distance. Zildryss lies looped around Britta's shoulders.

The water below is almost crystal clear, yet the reflections of the trees make it hard to see below its surface. Each shadow seems to represent the serpent's murky scales, making my stomach churn with unease. We round a few more bends, and something up ahead moves, catching my attention. I focus on it and find it's the Midgard serpent. The top of his scales rises above the water as he slides over a mound and into a large lake.

Chapter Nineteen

As if the serpent senses our presence, the ripples over the water's surface where he disappeared seem to slow down. Cloaked under the vast lake's surface, the serpent could have hidden there forever if we hadn't seen him enter. The lake isn't as large as Midgard's ocean, and I wonder if the serpent is coiled and lying still at the bottom. We pass over the lake several times, the dragons flying in the opposite directions, taking turns crossing through the middle.

By the time the sun has moved over the next mountain, Thor fidgets in the saddle behind me, making it hard to concentrate.

I growl. "Can you hold still?"

Thor groans. "I'm so frustrated. We saw it go in there, yet there isn't a ripple in the water." His twitching lessens.

Elan flies another couple of lengths before Thor

grumbles. "That's it." He yanks the ship's case from where it hangs on Elan's saddle behind him and moves to unclip the latch.

I panic. "What are you doing?"

He unfastens one of the clips and says matter-of-factly, "I'm opening the boat."

"Not while we're flying, you're not!" My voice goes up an octave. "You'll knock us out of the sky. Elan will be crushed by the weight."

Thor laughs, and I blink at him in disbelief. "Have you forgotten already?"

"Forgotten what?"

"The boat, *Skidbladnir*, changes size." With the case cracked open, he says, "Elan. Turn invisible, then lower closer to the water... please," he adds with a toothy grin after receiving a glare from Elan.

She does as instructed, flying just above the water, the wind from her wings stirring the surface.

Thor opens his case and tosses *Skidbladnir* at the water. "Pull up!"

Quickly, Elan turns in the opposite direction from the case then rises. The case flips open, a boat constructing as it falls. The hull of the *Skidbladnir* is completed before it lands upright in the water. The ship doesn't look much bigger than Thor.

Thor applauds. "There you go! Now, can you please lower near the ship, and I'll jump on."

As soon as Thor lands on *Skidbladnir*, he hits the magic spot, and the ship immediately grows to the size I remember it was in Midgard. With Mjollnir in hand, Thor peers over the side of the vessel and screams at the water, "Why don't you show your face and see who comes off best?"

Elan circles higher, remaining invisible and on alert. *Dragon scales! He's really feeling compensated with size. There is nothing like keeping it on the quiet and treating the serpent like the dangerous monster it is. Are you sure he hasn't been drinking?*

"I don't think so. Who knows what he's hiding in his canteen?"

Why don't you sniff it?

I screw up my nose. "Uh-uh! There's no way I'm sniffing that!"

In the distance, something stirs in the water. Scales rise stealthily above the surface, and beady black eyes fix on Thor. Slowly, the serpent slithers in the water. His focus narrows on Thor, his head rising farther the closer he gets. Soon the whole head is above the water, mouth open wide as he hisses, dripping black venom from his fangs.

I cringe at the black mixing into the water. "I hope the venom doesn't kill the fish of Vanaheim. Do you know how potent it is?"

Elan shakes her head. *Not a clue.*

The dragons circle Jormungandr's head, and the serpent arches, suddenly shooting farther out of the water and snapping at the dragons. Our flying friends hover out of reach, rising farther to ensure they are far enough away. Waves rock the ship when the serpent lands, splashing water over the side of the boat, drenching the god of thunder as he clasps onto the ship's side.

Something moves quickly along the edge over the other side of the lake. I'm shocked to see Jormungandr's tail flattening several trees along the bank. The serpent just fits in this lake, just like Thor thought. The knowledge makes my stomach drop. Thor will be in great danger in that ship with so little water.

Below, Thor has found his sea legs, bracing himself in a broad, balanced stance, Mjollnir held high as he summons the lighting. The serpent flips under the water, causing chaos over the surface. Fish breach on the shoreline in an attempt to escape, and as the serpent bucks, Thor loses his balance, toppling to the floor of the ship.

Drogon dives, horns first, and rams into the exposed flesh of the serpent. The serpent recoils, dragging Drogon and Hildr under the water before the dragon can dislodge his horns. Drogon digs his talons into the serpent, clawing his way to the surface, and takes to the sky, leaving a cascade of water showering from them.

Using the ship's rails, Thor clambers along the side and pulls himself up, hammer held firmly in one hand. This time the lightning comes, summoned by his call, and hits Jormungandr's tail resting on the bank. The serpent hisses, retracting his tail into the water, writhing underneath the surface. Unable to do anything besides ride the torrent, Thor grips the rails tighter as his ship lodges on the back of the serpent.

Thor summons another bolt of lightning, hitting some exposed flesh on the middle of the serpent. The monster thrashes harder, flipping Thor's ship out of the water. The ship lands with a thud as it catches on Jormungandr's body before slipping down to the water.

The serpent's large tail flicks across Vanaheim's surface, flattening trees as Jormungandr uses it as a brace and doubles back, heading toward the way it came. Large boulders topple over, some blocking waterfalls, others squashing foliage. The trail of destruction is devastating.

The ship is tossed around, sometimes by the serpent's flesh, other times by the turbulent water, making it impossible for Thor to brace long enough to attack.

Elan waits for an opening and dives down,

grasping Thor in her talons and carrying him to the shore. Thor's face is wan with tinges of green, and he staggers a bit after Elan places him on the ground, then she turns visible and lands, allowing him to climb on.

I clasp his hand with both arms, noticing with amusement that he's having trouble threading his foot through the stirrup to lever himself up. "What's the plan, my leader?"

Finally, he manages to secure his footing and kick a leg over Elan's back. "I think the best action is to get him back to Midgard. That way, it goes against my father's vision of him being part of Ragnarok."

I study the damaged shoreline and the lake rapidly losing its water. "Are we going to be able to do it without destroying Vanaheim in the process?"

Thor checks his hammer is hooked into his belt at the back then grabs onto my sides. "We can only try." Suddenly, he stiffens then jumps off Elan's back before she takes to the sky.

"What are you doing?" I ask.

He unhooks his hammer from the back of his belt. "I fight better down here."

Water splashing over the shoreline catches my attention. Jormungandr is leaving the lake and heading back along the river, except the water isn't deep enough for him to hide.

The ship whirls in the lake, pushed along by the serpent's movements. Surely he's not planning to return to the ship. There's no chance to use it in the river.

"Are you planning on fighting Jormungandr from the shore?" I ask in disbelief.

Thor shifts his hand on Mjollnir's handle. "I think it's best. I'm not used to riding dragons, and I would hate to get a dragon zapped by lightning or hit by the hammer."

Without warning, the serpent suddenly swerves our way. Elan launches into the sky, flinging me back, and I struggle to flow with the movement. Bracing my core and tightening the reins, I regain my posture.

Boots clopping softly on the moist ground, Thor runs with Mjollnir in hand and charges toward the Midgard serpent's head. The god spins, releasing his hammer at the serpent's head. Jormungandr changes direction at the last moment. The hammer hits his side and bounces back before returning to Thor's hand. A high-pitched hiss pierces the air, yet the serpent picks up speed and heads back the way he came.

Thor rereleases Mjollnir, hitting the retreating serpent. Jormungandr throws his head back, squeals a dreadful scream, and thrashes from side to side.

Thor jumps back, barely missing being hit by the serpent's body while catching the returning hammer.

The serpent changes his focus, circling his head to loom over Thor. Trails of black venom line the ground, and Jormungandr rears up, snaking his neck, ready to strike, aiming directly at Thor. He springs out, slashing faster than the mind can register, yet Thor manages to dart to the side, swinging at the same time. He releases his hammer, head first, back toward the serpent's ribs. The bone-chilling hiss the serpent releases sends involuntary tingles down my spine.

Jormungandr pursues the god single-mindedly. With hammer in hand, Thor runs up the river, drawing the serpent toward the Yggdrasil, occasionally looking over his shoulder to watch his pursuer's progress. When the serpent draws too close, the god rereleases his hammer, knocking him on the nose. The serpent rears up and hisses, expelling more black venom.

The next time, Thor conducts lightning, shooting it straight at the serpent. When the lightning strike hits its target, it gives the god a bit more distance. Thor spins, swinging his hammer. This time, though, he holds on to it. The hammer pulls his body, dragging him several leagues up the river toward the World Tree. When he lands on his backside, he bounces several times, skimming the surface.

I cringe at the pain the landing must have inflicted, but Thor seems undeterred and rises to repeat the process. Using this tactic, he manages to lure the serpent halfway to the Yggdrasil. Still, I have no doubt his luck will run out soon.

Drogon dives headfirst toward the serpent's tail. Hildr's sword is drawn. Magic burns in her hand as she presses her knees into Drogon's saddle and her back arches toward the sky. She strikes the serpent with a bolt of magic right as Drogon's horns ram into the serpent's hide. Jormungandr screams, twists, and flicks his tail, flinging Drogon out and leaving his horn marks in his flesh.

Tanda joins Drogon and dives down. She clutches a spot of the serpent's flesh with her talons while Britta jams her sword into the serpent. The Midgard serpent doubles back, swiping his tail, aiming for the two dragons, writhing and hissing a disturbing sound causing my whole body to shiver.

Zildryss pushes off Eir's shoulders and lands on the ground, not far from the bend in the Jormungandr's body. He arches his tail over his head like a scorpion and pokes it into the ground. Sharp rocks jut out of the river, poking into the serpent's flesh, jabbing him from behind, coaxing him along. Frantic black beady eyes search for the cause of the pain, unable to find the tiny dragon, only the rock causing him pain. He turns his focus back to Thor and slithers toward the god.

Elan swoops, scratching her talons along the flesh of his enormous body, giving Thor a chance to gain some ground. The god releases his hammer, aiming true to the serpent's nose. The serpent stops short, shakes his head, and then hisses before reinstating his chase of the god of thunder. When Thor catches his returning hammer, he holds it up, calling the lightning from the sky. Thunder clouds gather above Jormungandr, and lightning strikes not far behind the serpent, hitting the water and sending slight electricity shocks through the serpent's body. The serpent vibrates briefly before resuming his pursuit of Thor, eyes focusing only on the god. Jormungandr lashes out, missing Thor by a fraction, managing to knock his boots slightly, causing the god to stumble.

Naga swoops down in front of the serpent, distracting him from Thor long enough for the god of thunder to sprint out of the serpent's reach.

The dragons continue to attack Jormungandr's sides as the lightning strikes the tail, chasing the serpent out of Vanaheim. The destruction of Vanaheim is disheartening, yet we must continue, as it seems to be pushing him out of the realm. Suddenly, the serpent springs forward, lashing out at Thor. This time the serpent is too close for comfort.

Elan's wings halt, and we drop briefly from the shock as she realizes Thor is about to be struck. Elan's scream fills all of our heads. *Look out, Thor!*

Chapter Twenty

Thor attempts to dodge while gazing over his shoulder. The slash is so quick that we are all stunned. My heart skips a few beats, and I bite my lip, waiting for the outcome.

Jormungandr pulls back with Thor dangling from his mouth, the god's jerkin caught in the serpent's fangs. Thor kicks and sways, thankfully seeming unhurt.

Oh, no! That's not good. Elan turns invisible, and I adjust my cloak, ensuring every part of me is covered. She must be planning something. *Hang on!*

She swerves to the left then the right. My body leans significantly into her turns until she straightens and heads straight for Jormungandr's fangs.

The serpent thrashes, and Thor dangles oddly with Mjollnir in hand. If the situation weren't so severe, it would be comical. He swings his hammer and hits the serpent on the nose. Jormungandr shakes his head, and Thor dangles like a rag doll.

Drogon, Tanda, Naga, and Zildryss continue their attacks on the last half of the serpent, as Elan bides her time, hovering, waiting for the right moment to close in on Thor.

Elan's concentration through our bond is strong, and I leave her to her thoughts, not interrupting her to ask her plan. Instead, I wait, gripping her reins until my knuckles turn white and my hips ache from pressing my knees firmly into the saddle.

Jormungandr leers up, and Elan dives from above, straight at the serpent's mouth, where Thor precariously hangs. In front of the serpent, she jerks, tilting to the side, talons toward Thor, before fleeing the serpent's counterattack. Gazing over my shoulder, Thor swings wildly, still caught in the serpent's fangs, but now there's a significant tear in his jerkin where the fang pierces.

Elan grunts. *Dragon scales! I attempted to grab him, but he's still stuck there. That jerkin is made of thick leather.*

Thor swings again and hits the serpent on his head with his hammer. Jormungandr opens his mouth and lurches, adjusting his head in an attempt to swallow Thor. Somehow, Thor manages to use his hammer's momentum to get him away from the gaping mouth but is caught again on the serpent's bottom teeth.

Now, Elan! I cry through her bond.

The invisible dragon pumps her wings profusely, flying up to get to him. The branches on the trees nearby rustle in the breeze from her wings. Gritting my teeth, I wait for the serpent to notice the telltale sign. It doesn't seem to register, and I assume it's probably because the serpent is a sea creature and doesn't understand the different signs of the land and what they mean.

Jormungandr moves at the last second and Elan flicks her wings to shift closer yet still misses her chance to grab my leader. Her talons scrape along the serpent's jawline, eliciting a blood-curdling, unearthly hiss. He flings his head back, sending Thor flying directly toward his gaping mouth.

Fear stuns me for a second, as I worry Thor will end up in the serpent's mouth. Then I shoot a magic barrier in an attempt to block the gaping hole. Thor's jerkin unlatches from the serpent's tooth. He seems to hit my barrier then slide down it and hook back on the bottom tooth, leaving him dangling from the serpent's mouth again.

Hissing in frustration, Jormungandr continues his journey back toward the World Tree along the river, taking Thor as his prize.

The dragons continue their attack, swooping and dragging their talons along the serpent's back, wedging deep cuts along his thick reptilian skin. Despite the pain the dragons must be inflicting, he continues, seemingly happy with his prize.

Hang on! Elan says, and before I have a chance to take a breath, she swoops again, aiming for Thor. She tilts suddenly, her talons grabbing him around the legs, and she yanks, ripping him away from the serpent. His jerkin tears, and her wings labor to pull us into safety.

Gazing over Elan's side, I find Thor dangling upside-down by his legs. *Good job, Elan! You got him.*

The wind whips around us from the pressure of her wings, and I look back to see the serpent's beady eyes fixed on us, his mouth agape. He hisses. Black venom drips from his fangs.

With Thor still dangling from her talons, Elan flies toward the World Tree, not wasting a moment to look behind. *If Jormungandr is after Thor, he's going to have to follow me.*

His face beet red from the blood running to his head, Thor continues his attack on the serpent, hitting him with Mjollnir. "Put me down, Elan! I need to get the serpent."

Elan harumphs. *If I put you down, then you'll be the*

serpent's dinner. We've managed to aggravate him, and he will eat you in one bite.

"I can't let him get to Asgard, and he's caused too much trouble on Midgard and is out of control on Vanaheim. It's best to defeat him here," Thor argues.

Elan sighs audibly. *Look. In case you haven't noticed, this is a giant serpent. I get that you're almighty and tough and all. But even with us four dragons, Zildryss, and the Valkyries, you're still going to struggle against this massive thing. It's huge.* She pauses to let the words sink in. After a few wing strokes, she continues, *You need more hands. You need more help. You need more than just us to help you defeat it.*

His face a deeper shade of red, Thor smirks. "Aw. Eating companion. I didn't know you cared so much."

Elan growls. *Who else is going to give me free cows?*

Thor chuckles. "Probably many people, including Kara. But it's nice to know you care for me even though you're trying to disguise it."

Huh. Believe what you want. I'm doing this for Asgard, Elan says. *Where do you want to be put down?*

Thor smirks. "Somewhere close to the serpent."

You know you're annoying, don't you? Elan asks.

"That's my job. I'm a god." Thor studies the landscape then points not too far away. "Over there, please."

Chapter Twenty-One

Thor tilts his head up, and Elan slowly lowers him to his back on the indicated spot. He jumps to his feet.

Surveying the serpent, I tug on Elan's reins. "Elan!" When she doesn't respond, I tug again and call louder, "Elan! We need to move now!"

I sense Elan's body underneath me turn so she can look behind us in time to see Jormungandr's eyes focus through us, and he directs his body in our way.

I say through our bond. *He would be focussing on Thor, but our invisible bodies stand in the way. We need to move now!*

Thor springs to his feet, his hammer in hand and his legs braced in ready stance.

Jormungandr slithers closer, and Elan takes to the sky then dives, scraping the serpent's head with her talons. The serpent throws his head back and squeals, the breeze from the movement gushing our way as he narrowly misses Elan. Jormungandr shakes his head and returns his focus on Thor.

Thor thrusts his hammer up to the sky and drums up lightning. The lightning forks down, zapping the ground on both sides of the serpent. Another strike lands right in front of Jormungandr's nose. Dark patches of burnt grass and greenery are left in the lightning's wake. The smell of singed foliage seems to aggravate the serpent more.

Thor darts to the side and tries again. Lightning zaps down, aiming for the Midgard serpent's head. He pulls back just in time before the lightning strikes him.

Hissing, the serpent edges forward before coiling, setting himself up ready to strike. The god backs off, his hurried feet tripping over an Yggdrasil root. Quick on his feet, he manages to control his balance and continues to back up quickly.

The dragons strike from behind, ripping their talons into the reptilian flesh. Black blood oozes from the cuts. Jormungandr strikes, ignoring the dragons. It's almost like he's hurt so much that he doesn't notice the fresh attacks.

He swipes at Thor, and the god darts to the side in the nick of time. Thor spins, releasing his hammer with practiced precision, pummelling Jormungandr's head. The serpent rears up and hisses, each motion angrier and more frustrated.

Thor catches his hammer then spins and releases it, walloping the serpent's head to the side. Jormungandr shakes his head as though trying to regain his senses.

Thor taunts the serpent. "Come on, slowpoke. What are you doing? Come and get me."

The serpent halts shaking his head, pinning his beady eyes on the god, then lunges at him with renewed fervor. Thor barely slips past his attack. At the same time, he calls lightning to the spot where he once stood. The lightning hits the serpent, and it rears up, squealing, writhing, and hissing.

The smell of burnt flesh makes me want to gag. It's just as bad as rotting human flesh.

Shaking off his pain, Jormungandr strikes at Thor again. Then, Thor darts to the side and swings, hammer still in his grasp, hitting the serpent on his mouth. A sickening crack turns my stomach, and the serpent writhes, recoiling. He flicks his tail up and around, knocking everything behind him, flattening trees, and scattering large boulders.

Thor charges the serpent, runs up a boulder, launches onto the serpent's back, and smacks his head with Mjollnir. Another loud crack.

Jormungandr rears back, tossing the god off his back, sending him flying.

Elan leaps into the air, wings pumping profusely to reach Thor. The wind whistles in my ears as she dives, barely managing to catch him before he falls to the ground. Thor's body flops as she catches him. "Thanks, eating companion. You saved me again."

Anytime, Elan says. *Just remember you owe me a few cows when we get back.*

"Done and definitely done!" Thor says. "Can you put me down just over there, please?"

Are you ready for another bashing? Elan asks. *Anyone would think you're a glutton for punishment.*

"Haven't you heard?" Thor asks. "I'm all brawn and no brains."

Hmm. That sounds about right. Elan flies down to the location Thor indicated. *Here you go, brawns. Now, remember—don't think, then run straight into danger, just like you usually do,* Elan says cheekily.

Thor pets her side. "Thanks, Elan. You're always thinking of me."

No problem. I have your back. Don't forget that. She launches us into the air.

Thor dusts himself off just in time to see Jormungandr focussing on him again. It seems no amount of pain will put the serpent off attacking his prize. Thor rolls his shoulders then jigs them, getting them moving and warmed up. He then starts on his neck with his eyes on the serpent, readying himself for battle. He jumps up and down then twists and releases his hammer straight into the serpent. At the same time, all the dragons dive down, clawing at Jormungandr's back.

All the clobbering and tearing at the serpent's flesh must be extremely painful. Thinking of the pain he must be feeling pulls at my heartstrings, and empathy rises within me for the monster. I would hate to be on the receiving end of all those talons. Zildryss pokes a sharp rock from the ground to add to the pain, driving it straight into the serpent's underbelly.

Jormungandr shrieks, flicks his tail from side to side, then thumps it on the ground, narrowly missing the tiny lilac dragon. After expelling another mighty shriek, the serpent follows the river back toward the Yggdrasil, aiming straight for the hole in the trunk.

"Stop it!" Thor yells. "We can't let it get away from here. If he gets away, then we may not be able to find him before he causes more damage."

Thor summons lightning and forks it toward the tree, but it misses, causing the serpent to slither faster in the opposite direction. All the dragons rush to the tree. Despite all our efforts, Jormungandr makes it to the Yggdrasil and slides into the hole.

- Chapter Twenty-Two -

A ll the dragons dive toward the hole in the Yggdrasil's trunk, attempting to catch the tip of the serpent's tail before he completely disappears. Thor bolts to the tail tip, the last exposed part of the serpent, and slams it with Mjollnir. An almighty shriek bounces through the World Tree's trunk—the echoes distorting the sound, making it eerier than last time. My stomach churns. Yet the Midgard serpent doesn't stop. Instead, he flicks his tail, narrowly misses the dragons, and slams Thor to the side and into another tree.

The dragons attempt again to stop the serpent, only to end up pulling back, realizing our efforts are useless. We land.

Elan's golden eyes burn with determination. *We're going to have to wait for Jormungandr to slither away. There is no way past him and no way to draw him back onto Vanaheim.*

Drogon snorts out steam. *I agree. He takes up every inch of the trunk.*

Tanda furls her wings tightly against her sides, protecting Britta's legs. *He only fits because his bones maneuver to work with the space.*

Thor dusts himself off and joins us, glaring at the black blood trailing into the trunk. "This one is quite a monster. He's much more devious and persistent than any other monster we have battled."

Eir climbs off Naga's back and tends to Thor's injuries with her healing magic as Zildryss wraps himself around her neck and snuggles on top of her shoulders. "Where do you think he's going?"

"I'm not sure." Thor wipes the blood off his cheeks and other scrapes on his arms and knees, allowing Eir to attend his wounds. He investigates a tear in his pants. "That's the problem. I don't know which realm he's going to next. He could cause a lot of damage before we find him."

Britta stands next to Eir, peering down at Thor. "Do you think he's going to Asgard?"

Thor shrugs. "If he is, then Asgard is in great danger."

Hildr fiddles with the hilt of her sword. "We should ram a few of these into him next time. Maybe that'll slow him up even more."

Standing near Thor, I lean on one hip and rub my

forearm. "I'm not sure. The dragons' talons left deep gashes in the serpent, yet he still didn't stop attacking Thor. The strikes just seemed to make him angrier."

Naga sticks his head in the trunk. *Naga can't see his tail anymore. He must be gone.*

Thor limps to Elan's side. After climbing onto her saddle, I help him up, and he hooks himself in.

"You look a bit worse for wear," I say.

Thor grimaces and holds onto his side. "It's only a couple of scratches. Although, I must say, it's quite daunting being flung through the air like that."

I shake my head. "I can only imagine."

Eir mounts Naga, and we progress forward with Elan leading the way as she follows the trail of the dark blood. Slowly, she enters Yggdrasil's trunk.

I hope he's no longer in here. At least not facing our way, Elan says. *The last thing I want is to become that monster's dinner.* Her talons scrape along the inside of the trunk and slip at different spots where the venom, or sometimes water, makes it slippery.

A strange smell encloses around us, melding with the darkness mixed with the scent of wood. It's an acidy smell like venom, like a sharp, tangy smell that is probably the serpent's blood.

We take the trek slowly, giving me a chance to study the inside of the trunk. It's fascinating, and I'm amazed at how healthy the inside of the trunk looks lined with thick wood.

The other dragons' talons scrape behind us as they follow Elan. Darkness thickens around us, making it impossible to see. Slipping my hand under Elan's scale, I touch her soft flesh underneath and connect with her dragon sight. Instantly, I spot trails of dark blood from the serpent. "Is that the trail you're following, Elan?"

Elan picks up her pace. *Sure is. It seems like the best plan to work out where the serpent went. The blood seems to be everywhere, so it shouldn't be hard to miss when it stops bleeding.*

The tilt down is steep, forcing Thor and me to lean backward so our bodies sit straight. The additional scurrying behind us tells me that the other dragons are also picking up their pace to keep up with Elan.

Elan's wings are tucked by her side, securing our legs and making sure nothing rubs against them.

There's so much blood. Naga sounds daunted.

"I'm not surprised with the number of wounds we inflicted on the serpent. At least it gives us something to follow." Britta's voice cuts through the dark.

"It's a good thing," Thor says. "I would hate to miss out on catching the serpent or stopping it. My father would eat me himself if we missed this serpent and couldn't stop it from attacking Asgard. I'm not going to let this monster defeat us."

Zildryss suddenly makes startled high-pitched sounds. He dives off Eir's shoulders, lands on mine, and points to a path to the side with his tiny wing. I follow the direction and spot light through a hole in a branch. We redirect to the side, and the light slowly grows stronger. We must be approaching an exit into another realm.

I rub the little guy's chin. "Is that where the Midgard serpent went?"

Zildryss nods and points to the hole again.

Elan quickens her pace. *There's also a lot of the serpent's blood around the entrance. It's smeared almost everywhere. My guess is that it went through there too.*

We get closer to the hole. Her talons work harder as she hurries, pouncing from one side of the trunk to the ridge of the hole, and she perches on the edge.

Everything within me seizes, from my toes to my shoulders. I gasp. "He's gone into Asgard."

Thor slams his fist against the side of the trunk. "This is the worst outcome!"

Chapter Twenty-Three

E lan springs from Yggdrasil's trunk, and the other dragons follow, taking to the sky. It's surprising how quickly Jormungandr can move. We fly around for several minutes without any luck.

I call over my shoulder, "Where do you think he went?"

Thor rubs at the tear in his pants. "I don't know. If he's trying to look for rivers, he's going to have a hard time."

We search for a few more minutes, then Thor says, "If we can't see him around here, then perhaps the castle is his destination, or he's trying to sniff out my father."

Elan changes direction and heads for the palace. There are a few telltale signs of Jormungandr, and the blood trail seems to have dried up near the tree, occasionally showing a few splatters of the black blood.

I point in the direction of the black blood splatters. "It looks like that's where he's going."

Zildryss quirks and points ahead with his wing. Off in the distance, the serpent slithers toward the castle.

I rub the little guy's head. "Good spotting, Zildryss."

"Elan, can you fly faster?" Thor asks.

Without argument, Elan picks up speed. I glance back and see the other dragons catching up. They also have the Midgard serpent in their sights.

What's the plan? Elan asks.

"Hang on." Thor swings over to the side, hurling his hammer toward the serpent and catching it when it returns, narrowly missing Elan's wing.

Elan growls. *I don't think you should do that while you're on my back.*

"Sorry." Thor sounds embarrassed. "As I said, all brawn and no brain. I didn't really think that through."

Elan huffs.

"Can you put me down in front of him… please?" Thor throws in the *please* at the last moment when Elan shoots him a glare.

Elan increases her speed, gets in front of the Midgard serpent before turning invisible, and lands. She lowers, and Thor jumps off her back, his boots crunching on the rocks when he lands on Asgard's hard surface.

Thor lightly slaps the side of the invisible dragon. "Thanks, Elan." He takes off, Mjollnir in hand, summoning the lightning. Silver forks shoot down from the sky, hitting the ground directly in front of the serpent. Jormungandr pauses, and the god of lightning spins, releasing his hammer and clobbering the serpent on the back. The Midgard serpent's beady eyes land on him, ready to attack.

The dragons circle and commence their attack, similar to how they approached the serpent on Vanaheim. Jormungandr writhes with stress, flicking from one direction to the next, sending boulders rolling in the opposite direction. Suddenly, the serpent shakes, his body rising off the ground as though a deep vibration rocked the surface. The movement doesn't seem intentional.

I search for Thor. He, too, is bracing himself, with his legs spread and knees bent for balance. His gaze to the ground catches my attention. The whole ground is vibrating, not only the area around the serpent. Panicked, I search for the cause. It can't be the serpent. He didn't shake like this on Vanaheim.

After I search the area and come up empty, something catches my eye near the World Tree. Dread rises from the depths of my abdomen as red eyes glow hot out of the darkness of the Yggdrasil trunk.

"It's the lava monsters!" I yell.

It's not just them, Elan says.

"What do you mean?" I ask.

It's also the draugar, she says.

As soon as she's finished her sentence, the undead climb through the hole and clamber onto Asgard's surface.

Dread chills my whole body. "Can you tell the others, Elan?" The others are several feet below, too far for me to warn them.

I already have. Elan turns visible.

The other dragons, carrying their Valkyries, rise to the golden dragon's level.

"What do we do?" Hildr asks. "We can't fight all of them."

My dread deepens as I watch several lava monsters exiting onto our homeland, one by one, and draugar surrounding them, spilling onto the land like a rotten wave crashing onto the shore.

I chew my bottom lip, my mind spinning in all directions. Even though I am not their leader, they often treat me like one because I serve under Thor. *Any ideas, Elan?* I ask through our bond.

I suggest we find more dragons, Elan says. *I will fly to the dragon wasteland and ask them for help. Surely my mother won't let Asgard fall.*

Elan faces the three other dragons. *Can you please face them off with your riders for as long as possible? My mother should help us with all the dragons under her leadership.*

The dragons agree.

A slight peace edges into my soul, knowing that Elan's mother, Eingana, would come. She is a formidable fighter and has taught the dragons of the wasteland well.

"I should stay with the others," I say, listening to Thor slugging the Midgard serpent, unsuccessful in slowing down his progression to the palace. "Or at least I should help Thor."

Elan shakes her head and flaps her wings a few times in contemplation. *I agree the other dragons and Valkyries need your help, but I think you should go to Odin and explain what's happening. Get him to summon the help of the winged Valkyries and any other god around. Between these monsters and Fenrir, this is looking much like Ragnarok.*

A deep sadness fills me as I gaze at the faces of my friends and the dragons. I don't want to leave them alone in this battle. "I should be the one here fighting." I turn to Eir. "You and Naga should be the messengers. You can go to Odin and Naga to the wastelands."

Eir shakes her head. "Absolutely not! What do you think, Naga?"

It breaks my heart to think that this gentle blue dragon would be fighting these monsters.

Naga shakes his head, his blue eyes wide. *Naga thinks Elan should go. Elan will be our leader one day, and she should be the one to go to the wasteland. She shouldn't be the one to fight. Naga will always fight first before Elan.*

Eir strokes a gentle hand along Naga's scales. "Well said, Naga." She slides her hand under a blue scale and runs her fingers along his soft flesh. "And Kara has more experience with Odin, whether it be good or bad. Odin will be more likely to listen to her than some of her friends." The peaceful Valkyrie looks at all of the other Valkyries and asks Hildr and Britta, "What do you think?"

Hildr scoffs. "Of course we're staying and Kara and Elan are going."

The dragons and Britta nod.

Chapter Twenty-Four

E lan drops me off at the palace, and an urgency sets in. We've left our friends behind to fight those monsters. They're outnumbered and severely outsized. Each of them is battle-hardened, yet they're up against enormous odds. The lava monsters and draugar hadn't revealed their total numbers before Elan and I left. There could be hundreds.

My loyal dragon doesn't waste any time heading to the dragon wastelands—the sense of urgency weighs heavy on her also. Eingana, Elan's mother, is very wise. I'm confident she and the other dragons will come to our aid, especially since I convinced Odin not to enslave their babies to be used for battle practice. They need to be quick, though, or it could be too late for all of us. Worry twists my stomach into knots.

My footsteps echoing down the palace corridor are determined and urgent. Birger and Gorm said they hadn't seen Odin for quite some time, which left me searching the palace. My first stop is at the hall. It's often the place I find the leader of Asgard at this time of day. He seems to love placing people under his scrutiny and holding meetings or passing out sentences.

The farther I travel through the palace, the more my anxiety grows and turns the clacking of my feet on the stones into an ominous threat, luring the impending doom of Asgard and chasing me through the palace. My heart pounds against my ribcage as I hurry my footsteps. Reaching the corridor to the hall, I find Den in his usual place, guarding the double wooden hall doors.

I nod at him, not bothering to ask if Odin is busy, and barge through the large wooden doors, which groan on their hinges.

Den calls after me, "If you're looking for Odin, he's not here."

I stop midstep and quickly survey the room to find it empty. I turn back to the guard. "Do you know where he is? I need to speak with him urgently."

His blue eyes study me then tighten with professionalism. "He has gone to approach Fenrir."

Instantly, my cheeks turn clammy, and all the feeling vanishes from my arms. "What made him go to see Fenrir?"

Den's frown barely shows under his large horned helmet. "I'm not sure. Except, he was muttering, and I heard something along the lines of 'that stupid hound has escaped,' that he's 'seen it through the eye of wisdom' and 'must stop it before it happens.'"

I don't hold back my shock. "By himself?" Despite him being a confident warrior, it seems like a stupid move.

Den shrugs. "He seemed to be by himself. He was also muttering something about the magical lead not doing its job."

"Thank you, Den." I curse under my breath and bolt down the hallway.

Odin's crazy going there by himself or anywhere near Fenrir, especially now that the other monsters are here. Loki's three monster children are ready to attack Asgard. His fear seems to be coming true. Hel isn't here herself, but she has sent her minions, and it's not looking good. It appears like the buildup to Ragnarok, just like he predicted. After all our efforts trying to stop it, our time seems wasted.

I have to prevent Odin from going near Fenrir. The hound hates him with a passion, more than he hates me. And to go near him after seeing his lead failing is plain stupidity. He's serving himself up as lunch.

The clopping of my boots on the marble stones

chases me down the corridor in rapid succession. I charge toward the back of the palace. If Berger and Gorm haven't seen him recently, he must have used the back exit. The back way leads me through the cells where I once found Elan after she was kidnapped. I hurry past the cells, glancing at each of the occupants.

I stop in my tracks when I see one of the occupants is Loki. "You stayed in your cell."

Loki rises to his feet and walks to the bars. "Don't act so surprised."

I clasp at the bars. "It's not like you've stayed in your cell in the past."

One side of his mouth lifts in a smirk. "All right. I'll give you that. This time, though, I promised I would stay."

He did, yet I couldn't stop staring at him in shock. I honestly didn't expect him to keep his word.

Loki leans up against the bars at the front of the cell—one leg crossed over the other. His black leather jacket rests around his calves. "What are you doing down here?"

His casualness irks me, and I glower at him. "I'm trying to stop your monster children from destroying Asgard. I don't have time to chat." I hurry away, glad I don't have to deal with him right now.

He calls after me, "Can I help?"

Spinning on my heels, I narrow on him. "What are you going to do? It doesn't seem to make any difference if you're free or not. Your monster children still want to wreak havoc on this realm. They are determined to bring it down and destroy it." I grunt. "I have to go. Odin is trying to deal with Fenrir on his own."

Bolting from the room, I exit the palace and run down the back steps, following the path leading to the area where Fenrir is held. Adrenaline pumps through my body as I weave my way through the large boulders. After a while, my breathing grows ragged, blocking out the sound of my rapid heartbeat. I push on. I haven't seen any sign of Odin yet, and I'm worried he'll get to Fenrir before I get there.

This thought makes my feet move faster despite my exhaustion. Sweat gathers down my back, under my rattling quiver stacked with my bow and arrows, and my leather uniform squeaks because of the rapid movements. My sword, tucked between my quiver and uniform, presses hard against my back.

I wager that the area where Fenrir is tied remains half a league away. I squint at any form ahead, trying to find Odin. There hasn't been any sign of him so far. He must have left a while ago, and this concerns me. His elderly age would slow him down. Or, worse, perhaps he is already there.

I reach the mountain pass that separates the plain that encloses the area where Fenrir is secured with his lead pinned under a boulder. Thinking of the implications of having removed the stick from Fenrir's mouth, I curse myself. I've given Fenrir free rein to chomp at the god.

As I cut through the pass, the breeze carries a hound smell. Hopefully, this is a sign that Fenrir remains secured.

Yet I still haven't seen Odin. Perhaps the god hasn't come here yet. Surely, I would have caught up with him by now. When I near the edge of the boulders guarding the pass, I slow my pace in anticipation that Fenrir may be free. Nothing is stopping him from sneaking up on me if he is. We haven't had the friendliest relationship lately, and Odin may not be the only one Fenrir kills today.

Listening for any sound as I move forward several feet, I press against the side of the boulder for cover. I keep my eyes peeled. A rock crunches under my boot, and I curse.

A thundering growl echoes from around the corner, alerting me that Fenrir is there. He probably heard the crunch and is already on guard, ready to attack. I slow down, approaching at a snail's pace. I cross my fingers behind my back. When I reach the side of the boulder and edge my head around the corner, I catch sight of something and freeze. Odin stands barely out of Fenrir's reach.

The hound snaps, jumps, and growls, drool pouring out of his mouth as he pulls toward Odin. "Today is the day that I'm going to eat you."

Chills run down my spine. It's exactly as Odin described in his prophecy. Fenrir will be Odin's demise.

Loki's monster children have come together, and they're ready to attack. As predicted, the Midgard serpent attacked Thor, and it would be his downfall. Hel has unleashed her wrath.

My face has completely lost all feeling as I watch the scene before me. There is no doubt about it—this is the start of Ragnarok.

THE END

DESTRUCTION: book 9 in Thor's Dragon Rider series can be found on Amazon.

IF YOU ENJOYED ACCOSTED, please take a few minutes and leave a review on Amazon. Thank you. Reviews help authors find more readers.

Get updates & notifications of giveaways

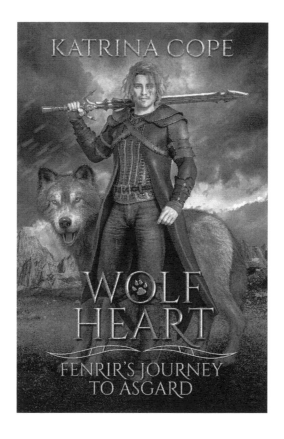

Would you like a FREE ebook?

Click here to get started: FREE copy of Wolf Heart: Fenrir's Journey to Asgard or go to https://BookHip.com/KQGGZF

Through this link you can sign up for my newsletter and

receive a FREE copy of Wolf Heart plus updates about my fantasy books, sales and notification of giveaways.

ACKNOWLEDGMENTS

Thank you to all of the creators of literature and websites who have spent time writing about Norse Mythology. Even though at times there has been contradicting information, it has been an interesting study. After all, of course a goat produces mead, and a dragon gnaws at the roots of the Yggdrasil, unhindered, threatening the existence of the nine realms attached to the world tree. Plus, there are many other "believable" tales told.

Norse mythology is such an impressive set of tales that I have incorporated some and invented others to create Kara and Elan's story.

I'm touched by the enormous amount of support I have received from my immediate family. My husband has been a helpful first reader and, at times, been an excellent motivator, with hints of ideas to help me through the blanks. The support from my three sons has also been overwhelming. They have spent years putting up with my head in the clouds, thinking about the next plot twist or story, along with many hours spent working on my books and keeping in touch with my readers.

A big thank you to my extended family, who support me being a book enthusiast.

A huge thank you to my editor, Stefanie B., for her editing and writing tips, and my proofreader, Laura K., for picking up the things we missed.

Thank you to all of my readers who have loved my work, and continue to read my stories.

BOOKS BY KATRINA COPE

Pre-Teen Books

The Sanctum Series

JAYDEN'S CYBERMOUNTAIN

SCARLET'S ESCAPE

TAYLOR'S PLIGHT

ERIC & THE BLACK AXES

ADRIANNA'S SURGE

~~~~~

Young Adult Urban Fantasy

Afterlife Series

FLEDGLING

THE TAKING

ANGELIC RETRIBUTION

DIVIDED PATHS

TRUTH HUNTER

Afterlife Novelette

THE GATEKEEPER

~~~~~

Young Adult Urban Paranormal Fantasy

Supernatural Evolvement Series

(Associated with the Afterlife Series)

WITCH'S LEGACY (Prequel)

AALIYAH

~~~~~

Young Adult Norse Mythology Fantasy

Valkyrie Academy Dragon Alliance

MARKED (Prequel)

CHOSEN

VANISHED

SCORNED

INFLICTED

EMPOWERED

AMBUSHED

WARNED

ABDUCTED

BESIEGED

DECEIVED

Thor's Dragon Rider

SAFEGUARD

PURSUIT

ENTRAPMENT

HOODWINKED

RELINQUISHED

SHROUDED

ASSIGNED

ACCOSTED

DESTRUCTION

ABOUT THE AUTHOR

Katrina is a best-selling author of young adult fantasy and middle grade / tween novels. Her novels incorporate action, heart and an intriguing plot.

She resides in Queensland, Australia. Her three teenage boys and husband for over twenty years treat her like a princess. Unfortunately though, this princess still has to do domestic chores.

From a very young age, she has been a very creative person and has spent many years travelling the world and observing many different personalities and cultures. Her favourite personalities have been the strange ones, yet the ones under the radar also hold a place in her heart.

Katrina's online home is at www. katrinacopebooks.com
    You can connect with Katrina on:
    Facebook Group

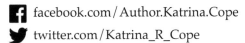

facebook.com/Author.Katrina.Cope

twitter.com/Katrina_R_Cope

instagram.com/katrina_cope_author

pinterest.com/katrinacope56

bookbub.com/profile/katrina-cope

Printed in Great Britain
by Amazon

83150300R00107